MW00623917

THE TRIAL OF ANNA THALBERG

EDUARDO SANGARCÍA

THE TRIAL
OF ANNA
THALBERG

Translated from the Spanish by Elizabeth Bryer

RESTLESS BOOKS

NEW YORK · AMHERST

First published as *Anna Thalberg* by Penguin Random House Grupo Editorial, Ciudad de México, 2021.

This translation of *Anna Thalberg* is published by arrangement with Ampi Margini Literary Agency and with the authorization of Eduardo Sangarcía.

First Restless Books hardcover edition September 2024

Paperback ISBN: 9781632063731
Library of Congress Control Number: 2024937644

Esta publicación se realizó con el apoyo que otorga la Secretaría de Cultura del gobierno mexicano, por medio del Sistema de Apoyos a la Creación y Proyectos Culturales, con el estímulo del Programa de Apoyo a la Traducción (PROTRAD).

This book is supported in part by a grant from the Mexican Ministry of Culture via the Sistema de Apoyos a la Creación y Proyectos Culturales, with the assistance of the Programa de Apoyo a la Traducción (PROTRAD).

This book is supported in part by an award from the National Endowment for the Arts.

Cover and interior illustrations by EKO
Cover design by Keenan

Set in Garibaldi by Tetragon, London

Printed in the United States

1 3 5 7 9 10 8 6 4 2

RESTLESS BOOKS
NEW YORK · AMHERST
www.restlessbooks.org

To Leslie, archimage.

To Vito, who believed in Anna
as much as or more than did Father Friedrich.

What more can the Devil do than throttle us?

MARTIN LUTHER

letter to Philip Melanchthon, June 27, 1530

WÜRTZ

Viser Frawnberg.

Heiding feld.

Buthiner thor

HERBI
POLIS, CÕ
MVNITER
WIRTZBVRG,
ORIENTA
LIS FRANCI
Æ METRO
POLIS.

Trutſch haus   S. Iacob.

Der Mair

Stift blaſij

THE TRIAL OF ANNA THALBERG

I

They came inside and chained her, not saying a word, giving no explanation. Anna Thalberg was crouched by the hearth stoking the fire when two men, short and robust like dachshunds, kicked in the door of her hut and assailed her, and she, like a deer surprised by hunters, leaped to her feet and widened her eyes as they drew closer, snatched the rust-licked poker from her hands, brandished before her face an arrest warrant bearing the bishop's seal as if it were a talisman, an amulet that would protect them from her dark arts and make their task of subduing her possible, restrained her hands behind her back, covered her head with an old hood, and dragged her through the crowd of onlookers who had already gathered outside the hut to see what the commotion was about

who watched as the men dragged the young woman out, lifted her into the air, and tossed her onto the wagon as if she were a bale of hay, a sack of tubers, much like the one in the kitchen from which she had taken three not long before, when she had set aside her distaff and started preparing dinner for Klaus, peeling them for the pottage that was sitting on the fire and that no one bothered to remove, not the men who seized her without warning nor the neighbors who went in to loot her meager belongings as soon as the wagon disappeared from view

a pottage that will boil over and blacken long before the embers die out, long before Klaus returns home from working the land and, for the length of his walk from the communal plots to the hut, finds himself continually besieged by the villagers' glances

glances that will disperse like flies when he meets them, only to regroup and perch on his back as soon as he turns his head, drawn to his walk home just as they were drawn to Anna's arrest, her shouts stifled by the hood, the men's indolent violence as they threw her onto the wagon and silently jumped in after her, at which time the wain made its way through the crowd of bystanders bearing witness with differing levels of pity, of outrage, of smiling satisfaction

> because finally she had been caught, finally justice was served, finally she would get what was coming to her, even if that poor man was made to suffer by consequence

the poor man who will step inside his hut, remove the cauldron from the hearth, and ask himself what the hell has happened here, who has taken his things, where on earth Anna is, why she has left their dinner on the fire, why, when he goes back outside to learn the answers from his neighbors, all of them avoid him, all of them pretend not to see him, just as they were deaf to the shouts of the young woman who, lying face-down on the wagon, begged for mercy or at least an explanation

> where are you taking me, who are you, what is the meaning of this

but the men said nothing, only whipped the horses and set off, followed by the neighbors' eyes, followed by the children and by the dogs running rings around the wain as it jolted across the hard dirt road toward Würzburg, a city Gerda had traveled to on foot the week before beneath the harsh estival sun to call for justice

because I shall not keep quiet, I shall
walk the seven miles to Würzburg and
throw myself onto the ground, I shall
kiss the boots of the examiners and
tell them what I've seen

what the people of Eisingen have seen

the redhead, the outsider, the one
with honeyed eyes like a wolf's, the
one with the speckled skin of a bane-
ful snake

what they believed they saw by moonlight, in the forest
shadows, and on the riverbank

the rumors spattering their talk as they bent over the
washtub doing the laundry

that woman, who else, the wife Klaus
brought back from Walldürn

what the women saw in their husbands' eyes when she
arrived in the village, what Gerda herself detected in the
eyes of her man

the very thing that roused her to walk the whole way to
the city, to the four-mouthed fountain outside the town
hall on whose parapet she sat to gulp water and watch,
but not comprehend, the slow revolution of the hands on
the tower clock, attentive to the people going in and out
of the building, to the crowd of laypeople and clergymen

among whom she recognized the thickset figure of examiner Melchior Vogel, at whose feet she prostrated herself to make her accusation

to blame her neighbor for evils as varied as the death of children in their cradles and the drought that had scourged the region for the past year, to convince him to send his lackeys to Eisingen to investigate and gather testimonies, to enter Anna's hut by force and throw her onto the crude board that served as a table, to chain her, cover her head with the old hood that smelled of fetid sweat and saliva, and drag her outside in front of her neighbors who moved not a muscle because they had gathered only to stare, not to intervene, not to prevent her from being thrown onto the wagon nor to remove from the fire the dinner meant for Klaus, who with his pitchfork on his shoulder and sweat pearling his forehead will watch the wagon pass from the plowing fields without suspecting that his wife is prostrate on it, and when he returns to the village will find his hut looted

his dinner ruined on the fire

his neighbors unwilling to tell him that men came from Würzburg and took her away in a wagon that the dogs and children tailed to the village gates where they lost interest and moved on to other things, other games, abandoning her to the goodness of God with no consolation other than prayer for seven miles of fear and confusion, of pain and a feeling of suffocation caused by the hood and the boot planted firmly on her back from the moment they departed the village until they crossed the stone bridge over the River Main, thinned by drought

stopping finally before the guard tower, by whose door stood Vogel, the examiner to whom Gerda had denounced Anna days before while they walked between the town hall and the market square toward the Marienkapelle, though Gerda will pretend to know nothing about what happened to her neighbor when Klaus knocks on her door and asks, will say she has not left home all day on account of her gout

poor Klaus, who will wander from hut to hut asking after his wife without receiving an answer, without anything but prevarications and looks of compassion, of mockery, of vengeance sated

because I accused her

because one afternoon, when Gerda was returning from the poulter, she found her husband leaning over the fence, observing the outsider with a glint that had never enlivened his eyes when he looked at Gerda, not even when she was younger and not so thick around the middle and had more teeth

I accused her, I walked all the way to Würzburg

all the way to the tower in whose shadows they locked up the prisoner, dragging her through several doors and up a stairway that ascended in a spiral to the heat of a filthy dungeon, where the air was barely breathable, to a small cell where the men threw her face-down after tearing off her hood but not her handcuffs, leaving her unable to break her fall with her hands, to soften her blow against the bare stone, a blow that freed her momentarily from her prayers and fears, from her efforts to understand, to breathe, from her hope of opening her eyes and finding herself back home

because this must be a dream

the idea arose suddenly in some corner of her mind as if the thought did not belong to her, as if someone had murmured it in her ear and after weighing it briefly she had accepted it as the most plausible, yes, it was just a dream, she was still at home and had drifted off to sleep, Klaus would be here at any moment, would touch her shoulder and chide her for nodding off before preparing dinner, then they would eat some hastily prepared gruel, would go to bed, and inevitably she would fall headlong into the same dream

I will be in this dark, stifling cell once
more, never again will I sleep in peace,
never again will I want to dream

and the intrusion of that thought made her break into laughter, not knowing why she could not contain it, and she cackled until the pain made her double over, making her captors lose their composure, exchange glances, cross themselves hastily, and run out of the cell in the direction of the examiner, that enormous ogre with whom Gerda had been granted an interview the week before, when she arrived in the city thirsting for vengeance, a vengeance that will find solace in Klaus's moving hither and thither about the village in search of his wife, in the closed doors that will not open to him despite his loud knocks, despite the growing anguish of a man who all at once will find himself alone in the middle of the night and in the middle of the withdrawn village, which will cower like a timorous animal to avoid all contact with him, making him think he has fallen victim to a spell, that he has been left all alone, that everyone in the village is dead, that Anna has died too or that he is the one who is dead and has returned

> that's why they are afraid of me, that's why no one wants to see me, no one wants to listen to me

and with that nightmarish feeling he will keep pounding on doors, will keep haunting the streets of Eisingen until a young man pulls him out of his anguish only to plunge him into horror when he discloses that she was taken to Würzburg accused of witchcraft.

Then he patted him on the back and left without a glance, left Klaus staked to the spot in the middle of the village not knowing what to do next, whether to go home or leave for Würzburg at once despite the hour, whether to wait until the morrow or start walking in the direction of the communal lands and leave the village, entreating the heavens to keep him from encountering a real witch

because not my wife, Lord, not my wife

or a werewolf like the one that had prowled the out-skirts of Bedburg a few years before, the rich farmer from

Bedburg who was dragged from his house in chains and hooded and taken to Cologne, where he was tried for lycanthropy, cannibalism, and Calvinism, and sentenced to death, as will happen in Würzburg to Anna, who at that hour, in the darkness of her cell, had surrendered to exhaustion and despite her fear, pain, and uncertainty was sinking into an imageless dream

a dream of darkness

of the mouth of a wolf, whose teeth Klaus feared encountering if he took the shortcut through the woods rather than the main road that skirted them, vacillating between walking two more miles and not exposing himself to as much danger or saving himself those miles but running the risk of falling into the maws of the many natural and supernatural beasts that roamed the forest depths by night

the bear and the vrykolakas, the werecat, also known as the lynx, and the dragon

if he decided to set out at once, it would be better not to think about any of this and just focus on Anna, on how she must be feeling so far from home for the first time since they married, whether she would be frightened or cold, whether she would be expecting him to do something to come to her rescue, to walk to Würzburg after the slumber hour even if he had no clue what to do on arrival, and in any case, the night watchmen would bar his entry until first light

but if he did not leave for the city right away his anguish would drive him mad at home, his anguish and his rage over his wife's bad luck and the greed shown by his neighbors, who had left nothing of value in his hut

only the cauldron with the blackened meal

old clothes, food for the moths

the broom, broken in two to keep a witch from flying on it

the hearthside stump on which Anna had been leaning when the examiner's men arrived

it would be better to walk and walk, thinking about something else but always on guard, alert to the sounds coming from the trees, prepared for any danger, with an ear to the crickets' and nightjars' song, the cicadas' whirring, the owls' hooting, a goat's nervous bleating in the distance

the sound of ceramics shattering on the ground

that sound coupled with a woman's curses right at the crossroads to the east of Eisingen, where by the light of the full moon Klaus saw Gerda hurling to the ground several clay utensils pilfered from his hut and then grinding those shattered pieces with her rough-hewn shoes

> so she doesn't return, so she never
> returns, may the Devil carry her away

for a lesson was not enough, that woman deserved to die at the stake as had the werewolf from Helmstadt, the one who devoured the Bürgermeister's daughter and turned out to be the village blacksmith, in whose workshop the young girl's splintered bones were found when they dragged him out and took him to Würzburg, where they burned him

Gerda herself watched him die, she could not contain her curiosity and on the day of his execution walked to Würzburg, wanting to see with her own eyes how they tied him to the stake and lit the bonfire with pages from his Lutheran bible, wanting to hear how the man begged for mercy only to curse and howl like a wild animal once the flames leaped across his gaunt and pale body, even wanting to fall victim to his final act of evil

> he looked at me and I lost my voice, I was struck dumb, nothing but breath left my mouth until he was dead, as dead as a doornail, may the Devil carry him away

as if by then the Devil had not yet carried the blacksmith away sometime between the crackling of the firewood and that of his bones, with the sizzling of his flesh, which filled the air with a sweet aroma that surely drew nearby demons just as milk did blowflies, making them eager to drag the doomed man's soul to the open mouth of hell, which must have devoured him with relish, just as Gerda hoped would happen to her neighbor after she burned at the stake and was judged by the Almighty, who is severe and just and who holds the two swords of judgment, just as she saw him represented in the western tympanum of the Marienkapelle in Würzburg the afternoon she walked through the market square alongside the examiner

apocalyptic Christ absolving and condemning the living and the dead, who return one final time from dust and ash, from oblivion and nothingness, who open their eyes to the white day for the last time to learn, finally, whether their earthly deeds have brought them reward or torment

divine Jerusalem or infernal Gomorrah

that was the exalted scene she gazed upon as she listened to Vogel's diatribe, before he passed through the doorway beneath the tympanum and joined the city council for the Holy Mass

two centuries before, the square, the chapel, and the surrounds had been a foul swamp where the Jews had their synagogue, whence they conspired with the Devil to sow the Black Death in the air, but the bishop learned of their perfidy in time and urged the residents to rise up against them, beating them with sticks until they were driven away or dead, until not one of them remained in the city, which was entirely Christian from that point forward

the same would be done now with the witches, who would be beaten, burned, flayed alive, and beheaded until not a single one was left in the region

> so will be done to your neighbor if
> enough testimonies substantiate your
> words, return to your village and con-
> vince everyone of what you have told me

and so Gerda was happy on her walk home from Würzburg that afternoon because she knew that everyone had seen it, everyone had suffered

the sour milk in the milking pails, the worms in the fruit, the lustful men like tomcats, devouring that horrid woman with their gazes

it would be easy to obtain their testimonies, easy to punish her neighbor, to plunge her into the monstrous mouth of hell, which devoured the damned on the lintel of the chapel Vogel entered once their interview had concluded, leaving Gerda searching for traces of her enemy among the condemned chiseled in stone, wanting to discover there, chained and being torn asunder by a big-eared, long-fingernailed demon, Anna, who will awaken early, emerging from the miasmas of sleep to the darkness of her cell, to the worn-out palliasse where she will lie with her back and arms aching, her wrists raw, incapable of anything but sobbing, praying, and beseeching assistance from the same God that Gerda invoked at the crossroads near Eisingen, asking that he condemn the witch so that the rains might return to the valley and her husband's soul might be saved

so focused on her prayer that she did not notice Klaus approaching until shards of ceramic crunched beneath his boots

receiving such a fright that before she could think twice she threw the last of the dishes at her neighbor's face and took off running toward the forest, beset by the shouts and curses of the farmer who pursued her between the trees for a good distance, pushing away the low branches and leaping over roots, bushes, and stumps, into one of which a copper dagger had been sunk to the hilt, an obstacle Klaus was not expecting and which made him trip

he fell and rolled on the ground, and though he leaped back up he lost sight of the woman's dull hair amid the foliage covering the slopes of Paukerhügel, Drummer's Hill

> keep running, you dirty Troll, when I catch up to you I'll smash your head in

he shouted as he dusted off his clothes and tried to get his bearings so he could make his way toward Würzburg from here, for if he returned to the village he would surely give in to the temptation to make good on his threat, may the Devil carry her away

he walked in silence through the woods, heading in the direction that habit indicated, not stopping to think, not searching for signs that he had kept to the path, which he had taken dozens of times since he was a boy, when he would go with his father to the city on harvest or carnival days, year after year he chose the route through the forest that meant he could save himself two miles until he thought the distance he had traveled was too great not to have reached the glade with the ruins of the old mill that marked the halfway point of the journey

that's where the Devil appears

his father would say, pointing at the foundations

he walked and walked through the brush, once more asking himself what he would do when he reached Würzburg, whom he could implore to rectify this mess, where he could find someone willing to assist his beloved wife who, at daybreak, lying in the dark cell, will try to understand what happened, what her abduction meant

the very thing the women whispered about at the market or in the square, where they gathered to listen to the town crier, who always had lists of names, accusations, punishments

Appela and Barbara Huebmeyer of Bad Waldsee, witches, burned at the stake

Dietrich Flade of Trier, sorcerer, strangled and burned at the stake

all the women of Korlingen, witches, strangled and burned at the stake

Peter Stumpp of Bedburg, werewolf, tortured on the wheel, flayed, dismembered, decapitated, and burned at the stake

things she preferred not to know, not to hear about, but everyone in the village seemed fascinated by such events and inevitably rumors of the arrests, the witch towers, tortures, and executions reached her ears

but she had nothing to do with witchcraft or any other abomination forbidden by the church, this could not be about that, it made no sense, there had to be some misunderstanding, and somebody would register it soon enough, somebody would realize and let her go

she will tell herself as much, that she has only to hold out, keep from despair, have faith that Providence will work in her favor, she will tell herself as much to calm down, and she will wonder too how Klaus is faring, Klaus who finally lost his composure and in desperation begged God for a north star in both his situation and the topography, for he was no longer in any doubt that he was lost, inexplicably he was lost in the forest he had known inside out since childhood, since he went with his mother to forage for mushrooms and if he lost sight of her had no trouble making his way back to the crossroads that led to Eisingen, where his dishes were now lying in pieces

how could I have lost my way

he reproached himself, perhaps the pursuit had taken him farther from his course than he had realized, perhaps he was worrying for no reason and was already close, but after walking another long stretch and searching in vain for the north star whenever he found himself in one of the forest glades, fear overpowered his spirit

it was plenilune and perhaps some witch, some evil spirit, even Gerda herself, about whom he had always harbored doubts, had placed a curse on him and that was why he had lost his way, that was why he could not find the windmill or Höchberg village, which given the time he had spent walking he should have reached by now, he should be able to glimpse the quarry that lay close to the village and signaled the final stretch of the shortcut

that is where the Devil appears

his mother would say, pointing at one of its berms

by now he should be able to see it, but since he had been bewitched, he was walking in circles, incapable of finding his way out, incapable of reaching the walls of Würzburg before the small hours as he had hoped

the silence surprised him still lost beneath the foliage

the sounds of the woods suddenly stopped, the crickets and cicadas stopped, the owl stopped, the seething mass of life surrounding him hid in the silence, and he sensed that something terrible was about to happen, was about to happen to him if he did not find his way out of the woods immediately, if he did not take off running and praying at the top of his lungs to ensure he had not lost his voice, that a werewolf had not stalked him, stealing his voice like had happened to Gerda in Würzburg

Vogel said as much to Gerda the day of the blacksmith's execution, after the old woman had gone to him and, sobbing, told him of the lump in her throat and asked whether it might have repercussions, whether she should fear the evil of that vile man now that he was in hell or if it was just a passing scare

> the werewolf strikes his prey dumb
> with his gaze, but you need not be
> afraid of him anymore, he no longer
> has any power over the living

he said as much and Gerda told everyone in Eisingen so that they might be careful, so that, if they ever lost their voice, they would hasten to the church to be saved

but Klaus was in the woods and there were no more holy places after Drummer's Hill, which he had left behind hours earlier, ahead were only places frequented by the Devil, places where he appeared in the form of a toad or rooster or dog or maiden or youth or even in his true form, accursed places where so many had seen him, everyone had come upon him at some point in the forest or by the river, on the paths, on the outskirts of the village, and sometimes within it too, in the tavern or the house of ill repute

> everyone has seen him except me, and I don't want to see him
>
> for the love of God, I don't want to

and so he began to run with all the vigor his terror lent him, he ran, aware as never before that he was made of flesh and could become prey for wild beasts and vermin, he ran without another thought for his wife or Würzburg or his looted hut or Gerda breaking his crockery at the crossroads to ensure Anna would never return

> so she burns and writhes at the stake, may the Devil carry her away, and if he cannot, may he drag her off

he ran, convinced that it was gaining on him, that he had become another creature's quarry and what was pursuing him was so close that he would be caught before he reached the forest fringes, which he could now discern ahead, beyond two thick trees, between which was a narrow glimmer

convinced he had no time to go around, he threw himself through that opening, scraping his head, his shoulders, his arms, his hips, and his legs in his frantic struggle to escape, to plunge forward, to fall to the ground and drag himself far from the vegetation, whimpering like a baby, turning his distorted face without making out his pursuer, without finding anything hounding him

nothing but the trees he had just passed through

nothing but the tears that flooded his vision for the long interval he lay there, hugging his knees, trembling like a puppy until he heard the roosters heralding the dawn

only then did he rise to his feet and see, just a few strides distant, the dry riverbed of the Kühbach, which continued on until it reached the River Main, beyond which, in the far distance, he could make out Our Lady's Hill and, at its peak, the Marienberg Fortress bathed in the first light of day.

III

From over the hill flowed the waters of the River Main, and on the far bank of the Main rose Würzburg, shielded behind a twelve-gated wall whose shape deliberately suggested a miter as a perennial reminder of the bishop's authority over the city and its inhabitants, over the houses and churches and gardens and workshops and mills and markets and squares and streets and alleys, over the wall itself as well as its moats and towers, within one of which Anna had been lying in the dark for hour upon hour, intoning prayers until she had emptied them of meaning, until she had quelled her fear and anxiety and the only things keeping her praying were the inertia of her thoughts, the ecstasy the meter had lulled her into, and her need to pass the time, for in the gloom she had no way of measuring or calculating how many hours had passed since she had been locked in that tower, if it was day or night, if a few hours or many days had gone by, if time had congealed like the dense air inside her cell, if the minutes only dragged themselves as do slugs along their sticky secretions, prompted by tedium or anguish

but time, though it may drag, never halts

time kept rolling, and Anna was able once more to apprehend it when the door creaked open and in came a coarse-shirted, black-stockinged servant who freed her hands from their handcuffs and set down a greasy-rimmed bowl, inside of which wobbled a mutton stew that drove off her appetite instead of whetting it even though she had not eaten since the previous afternoon, when she chewed a little of the carrot and radish that she had sliced for the pottage meant for Klaus, who, like her, will not have eaten since the day before, and who, much to his dismay, will be unable to silence his stomach's growling when, after daybreak, Vogel deigns to see him after making him wait three hours while he makes up his mind to leave his bed and his quarters two hours during which he had breakfast and listened to the Holy Mass in the Cathedral dedicated to Saint Kilian, patron of the city and its first Christian martyr

one more hour after he stepped inside the building adjoining the guard tower and finally decided to call Klaus to the underground chamber he had made his office, so austere that its only furnishings were a chair, a desk, and atop it a wooden *Ecce Homo* from the late Tilman Riemenschneider's workshop, so cramped that the examiner could surely hear the peasant's intestinal gurgles so clearly they could have been his own, augmenting his disdain for the grime-covered man in tattered clothing whose plea on his wife's behalf will be devoid of eloquence, with truncated phrases, yelps, and ditherings that will only serve to exasperate him since not even Saint Kilian himself, he who convinced Duke Gozbert to embrace Christianity, could persuade Vogel to free Anna

because she is a witch, young man

and the cell door had barely closed when his lackeys heard her cackle as if the prison and fetters amused her, he himself had gone up to hear that demonic laugh, that derision aimed at the examiner and his men, the church and Our Lord, convinced as she was that the Evil One's protection would allow her to prevail, but Vogel could vow that she would have no command of her evil arts while imprisoned in the tower, and just as all who entered only ever left in the direction of the bridge or bonfire, never again would she have the opportunity to do evil, so it had been since the bishop, on his nephew's advice, had consented to the southeast guard tower becoming the holding place for witches caught in the territory under his authority

none of the prisoners brought by the lackeys from the four corners of the bishopric had returned to the lay world

no one who knows her will see Anna again until the afternoon when she is taken to the pyre after confessing her guilt, after accepting all the atrocities she has committed for the greater glory of Satan

practicing witchcraft, lying with demons, and inciting the men of Eisingen to fornication

provoking and prolonging the drought that destroyed the grain in the fields and the cattle in their folds and stables

nobody will see the young woman until that afternoon when, her arms dislocated, her back broken, her stomach bloated, and her fingers mangled, she declares herself guilty and accuses other villagers of attending the Witches' Sabbath, providing their names to the authorities

nobody will hear her until she is taken to the market square and tied to a stake that stands in the spot where in spring the May tree with its green crown will be raised there Anna will scream as she burns in front of Klaus, who with his head hanging in shame could do nothing to hide the sounds his belly was emitting in the tiny office, stomach rumblings that hours before had tormented Anna too, obliging her to stifle her repugnance and reach out a hand toward the greasy plate only to draw it back suddenly, having brushed the back of a rat that was scarfing the mutton

she retreated to the opposite corner with her skirt pressed between her thighs, wondering how many others must be scuttling around, how many others must be trying to eat their fill of mutton only to find themselves still hungry

that is how she will stay for a long while until they come for her, until Vogel, fed up with hearing the groans emitting from Klaus's stomach, sends him out of his office to continue the proceedings against the woman despite the arguments the peasant babbled on her behalf

because not my wife, my lord

since their marriage day, night after night they had shared a bed, and if in the early hours a strange noise wrenched Klaus from sleep, if the furniture creaking or the dogs marauding the streets caused him to wake in a cold sweat, praying the Our Father, fearful that without the hut would be a revenant or a witch, Anna was always lying by his side, sleeping calmly, like an angel like a demon, more like it

responded Vogel, for it was well known that when witches escaped to the forest to consort with Satan, they would offer their marriage bed to a succubus that would lay with their husbands, steal their semen, and offer it to the old enemy so he could spawn more demons in witches' wombs, for the Devil is sterile, he does not procreate, he is incapable of generating life

it happened every coven night

he continued, picking his nose and examining the findings, talking as if he were speaking to himself and not to someone else, for nobody important was standing before him, only a hungry and ignorant peasant to whom it was necessary to explain the rudiments of demonology

just a poor devil whose stomach would not stop growling for the duration of the interview, as did Anna's, still demanding food when the tower servant and Vogel's two men entered her cell again, handcuffed her, hooded her, and dragged her down the stairs through the tower entrance, until they came to the bridge over the River Main where the city court met to pass judgment on delinquents and criminals

without warning they removed her hood, dazzling her with so much sudden light after hours of gloom and utter blackness, leaving her blind with clarity she blinked and slowly began to discern amid the whiteness the other accused who were appearing before the court that day, the semicircle of dignitaries assembled there to judge them, the centenary bridge of stone over the eternal river on whose eastern bank they were standing, and in the distance, beyond the arch of the gate over the bridge, the Gothic spires topping the orange towers of Saint Kilian's, the vermilion spire of the Marienkapelle, the closest tower of the city hall with its clock and its bay window, and on the other side of the River Main, upon Our Lady's Hill, the trapezoidal hulk of the Marienberg Fortress, in whose contemplation she lost herself until she heard her name on the lips of the promoter of the cause

> Anna Thalberg, wife of Klaus Thalberg, native of Walldürn and resident of Eisingen for the past two years, has been accused of attending the esbats on the outer edges of the Blutsee-Moor and the Great Sabbath on Walpurgis Night, celebrated in the Harz, where she traveled mounted on a goat to dance with the Devil until she fell to the ground in exhaustion and thereupon joined with him *per Angostam Viam*

she was accused, thus, of witchery, of stealing the host and using it in blasphemous rituals though Klaus swore to Vogel that his wife was a devout Catholic, that she had never missed Mass, that she had always fulfilled her vows and fasts and had confessed her sins every Sunday and on feast days to receive the body and blood of Our Savior, all of which could be attested by Father Friedrich, priest of Eisingen, as soon as he returned from Bamberg, where he had traveled weeks before to care for his moribund brother

he could tell you so, my lord

but Vogel appeared unyielding, not even Saint Kilian himself, who convinced Duke Gozbert to repudiate his wife Geilana for being his brother's widow, could persuade him

because devotion was no proof of innocence, witches were known to appear excessively pious to disguise their turpitude, they purported to be good Christians, good wives, and good neighbors while beneath their masks they were but seeking the flock's perdition

they purported to be good mothers, too, though in that regard, noted Vogel, Anna had been even more iniquitous, for she had failed to give birth to a living child, it was documented in the testimonies that at least three times she had bled halfway through a pregnancy, everyone in the village had heard about it they knew too about her excursions to the woods, and that she spent entire afternoons there, perhaps on those forays she met with her diabolical lover and delivered him her offspring as sacrifice

there were more than enough testimonials, his wife was a witch and for that reason would be condemned, and after catapulting the ball of mucus to the floor with his middle finger, Vogel dismissed Klaus with a wave of his hand and returned to his paperwork, worrying no further about the peasant who remained rooted to the spot, begging in a soft voice and with his gaze on the floor until a new barrage of stomach cramps forced him to leave the office with no other plan but to go back to Eisingen to await Friedrich's return and ask for his help and counsel

and to satiate however he could the feral hunger that was making him double over and sniff the air in search of something to cram into his mouth

he left Würzburg through the mirror gate and crossed the bridge over the Main before the court was to assemble, before they were to remove Anna from the tower, stand her before the council, and read out the charges against her, before she was to look in horror at the judge, the promoter of the cause, and Examiner Vogel, the first as short and the second as scrawny as the third was tall and burly a dwarf, an elf, and an ogre, charged with determining whether or not she was a witch

> I am not, my lords, I believe in one God, the Almighty Father

she began, but Vogel interrupted to remind her that all women, according to Saint Paul, should remain quiet

they made her stand aside while they read out the charges against the other accused and carried on the trials that had already begun, the long hours weighing ever more on the young woman's feet until the last trial was concluded and a man was found guilty of murdering his brother-in-law

after a brief deliberation, the court sentenced him to death by water

the guards lifted him into the air and took him to the parapet of the bridge, and darkness drew over Anna once more

again they hooded her and made her start walking toward the tower

she could not see what was happening but she heard the man's shouts, the splash of his body against the river water, and nothing more

the scream, the splash, and then nothing more
nothing more.

IV

Near Zobel's Pillar, Klaus's strength abandoned him, his vision blurred, and his ears closed as if black storm clouds were hovering above his head and the people alongside him bustling to and from the city were gesticulating and moving their lips without making any sounds, as if the huge wolf of the night were lying in wait nearby, ready to spring upon any one of them

but it was daytime, the sky was clear, and the people were chatting with utter normality some passersby looked disdainfully upon him, assuming he was an inebriated beggar who had suddenly lost his balance and ended up at the foot of the column, leaning against it as he waited for his malaise to recede and to find himself in a well enough state to be on his way, but one man shoved him away from the pillar, reproaching him for the lack of respect he was showing toward the site where fifty years before a bishop had been mortally wounded

with great effort he continued walking down the street, leaving behind the fishermen's quarter and coming out onto open land once more, where a second dizzy spell made him fall flat on the grass, and this time he started pleading on the inside, calling out for help to Father Friedrich, who at that hour was crossing the Steiger Forest on his journey homeward to Eisingen after burying his brother amid great pain and sorrow

> and yet, he who has been good, he
> who has led a just life knows when
> death is nigh

he told himself, carrying a sword and laden with grief that had been bequeathed to him by his brother along with a sack of coins, wanting to believe that the Lord had allowed a just man to know the end was nigh so he could get his house in order, bid farewell to his friends, bless his family, and prepare for the *postrer trance* ready to bask in eternal glory, while those condemned to hell are caught by surprise, the end comes to them like a thief stealing forth in the night, or like a bird of prey that dives into its quarry from a great height and never misses

and Joachim knew ahead of time, he sensed death's approach and sent his servant to Eisingen to notify Friedrich, to ask that he travel to Bamberg to assist him in his dying moments and hear his final testimony, which began with the room crowded and ended with only Friedrich because friends, neighbors, and onlookers had withdrawn aghast at the tirade against everything sacred, against the empire, the crown, and the church, even against God himself

but he knew that death was nigh

if the Lord had abhorred him, he would have smitten him as with a lightning strike

as had happened to Anna and Klaus's door, which the men's kicks had dislodged from its doorjamb

as happened to the rabbits Klaus found sniffing the air and rootling the dirt in search of their burrow until Klaus fell upon them

as happened to Anna as she stood before the equip-ment made of wood and iron that had been arranged across the floor and hung from the walls in the torture chamber, mocking all imagery of hell, where they took her after the proceedings on the bridge

they removed her hood once more and, by the light of the torches, their tarry odor mixing with that of the dry blood and shit emanating from the floor and walls, she distinguished those fixtures, manifestations of pure evil, and, unable to abide the sight, she fainted to the floor

> Joachim would have been smitten thus had God not had his name written in the Book of Life

that was what Friedrich told himself by way of encouragement while his wagon crossed the forest, while he gazed unseeing at the rays of sun filtering through the dense foliage, the play of light and shadow demarcating a pattern of such beauty that it seemed to testify to the existence of God, the very existence that his brother called into question before he expired, facing the wall as did the Jews after refusing to receive the Extreme Unction, resolved not to die in the bosom of a church that had washed its hands of its Germanic flock, leaving her at the mercy of the demon Luther and his legions

he died renouncing the God that had allowed the Antichrist's princes to sack towns across the Holy Empire, had allowed Albrecht Bellator, the worst of them, to invade the Prince-Bishopric of Bamberg, set fire to every village he came upon in his march toward the city, and run his sword through innocent and unarmed people, Joachim's sons among them

during the razing of Kürnach, the two boys ran to the church seeking refuge, but the Bellator's troops kicked in the door and dragged them out, slit their throats, and hung them upside down from an oak, and nobody bothered to cut them down, nobody

for five days and their moons, nobody

Hermann and Joseph, my sons, bone
of my bones, flesh of my flesh

forsaken by God despite their being steadfast and immovable in their faith, no less Catholic than the Caesar Charles who, despite the Bellator's horrendous crimes, gave him his hand, pardoned his vile deeds and apostasies, and allowed him to battle at his side against the French, the killer's then-enemies, soon-to-be friends, for the Bellator would choose to serve them later, once the emperor had abdicated the crown and withdrawn to distant Spain to bury himself alive in a remote monastery in the highlands, where he devoted his final years to lying motionless inside a coffin and directing his own funeral rehearsal day after day, forcing the monks and hermits to pray litanies and responsories for his soul's eternal rest while the bells pealed in mourning, as demented as the shrouded monarch himself, as demented as his demand that God take his soul

having long forgotten his youthful promise to devote his kingdoms and dominions, his friends, his body, his blood, his life, and his soul to bringing an end to Protestantism

having surrendered to that ridiculous imitation of the Empyrean, where angels praise God without end while the celestial spheres peal their music, demented

convinced, despite his broken promise, of having fulfilled the mission that the Lord had placed him on this earth to accomplish, as convinced of this as Luther, as Pius IV, as convinced of this as Jesus himself

his Caesarean Majesty, lying in his coffin bathed in the candles' flickering light, his eyes closed tight, holding his breath every so often, wondering, as might you or I, how it must be, how it must feel, whether it is like falling or soaring or sleeping or even dreaming, he forgot about those among his Germanic subjects who remained faithful to the empire and to the papacy, condoning through this neglect the massacres the Protestant princes were committing across the Holy Empire over minor differences of opinion about how the same God should be worshipped

the God whom Klaus begged that Friedrich would be back in Eisingen, where Klaus was now headed at great speed, restored after his bite to eat, crossing the woods at a trot with one of his kills limp between his jaws

the same God whom Gerda was thanking from the bottom of her heart for the favor granted, singing for the first time in years as she prepared a pottage, as she peeled potatoes and stoked the fire, overcome by the good fortune of knowing that the neighboring hut was still empty

the God to whom Anna was clinging so as not to faint again as the executioner and lackeys delighted in describing how exactly the thumbscrews, the stork, and the cat's paw worked

the God whose clemency Friedrich was seeking when he made the case for his brother, when he asked that he forgive him and find mercy in his heart for all the suffering he experienced after his sons' murder, and his certainty that Joachim had sensed death's approach gave him hope

> because only the righteous, never the
> wicked

he decided to make a detour toward Kürnach before reaching his village to visit the tree from which his nephews had been hung

in those days Friedrich was newly ordained and exercising his ministry in Münnerstadt, a city to Würzburg's north, where he had invited Joachim to help with the ironwork needed for the church while his nephews, who were leaving adolescence behind, were left in charge of the family forge

that was why they were alone, that was why their father did not die alongside them

Joachim and Friedrich had to leave Münnerstadt after the Count of Henneberg, city regent, converted to Protestantism

they left that city in the belief that they were leaving the Lutheran heresy behind, that they were returning to the protective bosom of the Catholic church, but upon arriving in Kürnach they found half the town razed, the house and forge plundered

dinner rotten on the hearth

the neighbors reticent, unable to meet Joachim's gaze or respond to his terrible question

my sons, where are my sons

an adolescent led them to the massacre site, a tree into the bark of which Joachim drove a cold chisel after throwing the other tools in his apron to the ground, before throwing himself down to cry and tear out his hair

warmth of my life, Word of God in the mouth of time

they cut them down together and buried them separately, the neighbors made excuses, indicating the killers' warning

> the bodies must remain hanging
> here as an example to all those who
> would use the forge in support of the
> Bellator's enemies

yet not a single sword had been forged in that smithy until the week after the boys' obsequies, when Joachim crafted the weapon that Friedrich now carried on his lap, dashing to Bamberg with it, seeking vengeance or death, only to find, when he reached the city, that the invaders had been repelled already, a situation that recurred in Forchheim, in Hof, in Kulmbach, and in every Bavarian city, town, and village he passed through on his hopeless pursuit, in his desperate race to reach the front and fight

in each place, he found only the jubilation of victory against the apostates, which several months later became definitive when Albrecht fled for France

the blacksmith had no choice but to retrace his steps, but the burden on his shoulders grew heavier the closer he came to Kürnach such that he stopped in Bamberg and lived there until the afternoon he declared to the mourners gathered around that he had finally managed to exhume the bare bones of religion

fear and impunity

> for there is nothing behind the veil
> but those cruelties, for God is naught

but guarantor to the worst crimes, the
last hope man clings to when faced
with the terror of being gone forever
in his will, when the executioner grips
the ax and the warrior the sword
into God's hands the victim commits
his spirit in the hope of seeing the
light of another day
in his name anything is permitted,
and with his name man tries in vain
to divest death of its sting, but it
always catches up with him, always

as just then it caught up with Joachim, who could go
no farther, overcome as he was by the Reaper

he halted midphrase and died

he gritted his teeth, went silent, and died

he opened his eyes, which intense pain had kept
closed, and died

he opened his eyes, looked at Friedrich as if he had
forgotten who he was, and died

he looked at Friedrich and asked

have you ever seen horses copulate

and died, his eyes open

with a tremulous hand, Friedrich lowered Joachim's
eyelids and arose from the floor where he had been

kneeling by the bed, approached the hearth to light the mortuary candle, and took from between his brother's hands the cold sword he had forged in those bleak days, raising a prayer to ask God to disregard his senseless tirade and pardon his sins, for in a sense he had died decades before, alongside his sons

he had died alongside them in that monstrous end on the tree that Friedrich approached after leaving the road, feeling around for the spot where Joachim had sunk his cold chisel, intending to thrust the sword there again, but after two attempts he was persuaded that he did not have the necessary strength

he wrapped the sword in its goatskin and, after tossing it aside, threw himself to the ground, stretched out his arms in the shape of a cross, and, sobbing, prayed the Commendatio Animae against the express wishes of his brother, then he got to his feet, took hold of the sword, and returned to the road, where he resumed his journey toward Eisingen, ruminating despite himself on the blasphemous barrage that his brother had issued in his death throes while the world, indifferent, kept turning, having already forgotten Joachim and his sons, who were resting belowground, no longer in peace.

V

To wake her they tossed water into her face, water that reeked, as did everything else in that chamber of horrors, the air she breathed, the floor she was lying on, the dirty torture instruments strewn around

two hundred different samples of blood crusted the rust and stained the timber to ocher

the blood of two hundred unfortunates who had passed through the dungeon before Anna, whose flesh had tested the efficacy of the Judas cradle, the wooden horse, and the pendulum two hundred souls that were first shoved out of their vessels in that wet, fetid place, as wet and fetid as Anna's face after she was reawakened between gags and gasps by the bucket, which brought her back to the executioner's harangue, to his demonstrating the workings of the wheel and the rack and Saint Elmo's Belt, to his warnings and recommendations

she would be better off confessing at once and thus escaping the worst of the torture, better off accepting the charges now, for in any case she would never be permitted to leave the chamber without first confessing her sins and misdeeds

he had enough instruments at hand to break her bones one by one and lacerate every inch of her skin, every item in that place had been fashioned expressly to break the will of the most headstrong witches

I am not, my lord

she would be better off backing down from her evil insistence and admitting her guilt before the examiner who, lurking in the doorway, was privy to the scene, his hands behind his back and his head thrust forward like that of a vulture

because once my task has gotten underway there will be no mercy

he would put her thumbs inside the vice and turn the screws until her nails broke and her pads ruptured he would place the stork's iron rings around her neck, wrists, and ankles and leave her immobilized with her knees to her stomach, and if at first she experienced only a slight discomfort, as the hours passed she would be overcome by cramps far worse than those of childbirth, and they would not cease, they would not let up

and that would be just the beginning

he would hang her by her wrists from the hook and tie several weights to her ankles until her arms were pulled from their sockets

he would use the cat's paw to rake slivers of skin from her breasts and then he would rub the wounds with salt, so that demons, which find salt so offensive, would never again lick her breasts

the executioner would do all this and more

he would make her suffer until he left her deaf and blind, until he had made of her but a screeching throat, an unabating howl, a torn cavity, and a pulverized phalanx, he would make her wish for death, though if she intended to die unrepentant then death would not be the end of it, for she would be condemned to hell for ever and ever, where only God knows what torments he conceived in his infinite wisdom as eternal punishment for the damned

she would be better off submitting immediately and accepting her neighbors' accusations, compiled by the

servants and presented before Vogel as proof of malfeasance and cruelty, of perverse tongue and evil eye

irrefutable proof of witchcraft

I am not, sir

Blaz Fusch, native of Eisingen, dairy farmer by trade,
blames the accused for inciting a heavy hailstorm that
felled two of his cows after she argued with him over the
price of cheese close to two years ago, when she moved to
the village as a newlywed

I have known no man other than my
husband

Ebba Nussbaum, wife of Kiefer Nussbaum, native
of Helmstadt, blames the accused for the miscarriage
she suffered while she was visiting her mother-in-law
in Eisingen, days after the accused had put her hand on
her belly without warning, while they chatted about the
future delivery

never have I lain with another man,
much less with the Devil

Kunigunde Hemmer, native of Eisingen, old maid,
alleges that one morning she found her dog eviscerated
behind her hut and insists that the accused is to blame
because, the afternoon before her macabre discovery,
on returning home with her laundry she surprised the
accused playing with the animal

Hemmer does not understand the motives behind the incident, if the accused needed the entrails for some poultice or potion, if she did it out of mere vengeance for being chased off the day before, or if she wanted to be rid of the dog because it was a stupendous mice hunter and she feared it might catch one of her familiars by mistake

> whose member is said to be as long
> and as thick as an arm

Gerda Bauer, native of Eisingen, hen and duck keeper, submits that one night she saw the accused flying over the village rooftops, riding a wild goat back to front, the animal's horns long and curved enough that she could reach around them and hold on with just the crooks of her arms while she kept her legs apart, as if she were ready to receive a man, and floated toward the Blutsee-Moor

> and hard and cold and forked, and
> he has it at the back, between his
> buttocks

Bertha Neuden, native of Eisingen, baker by trade, swears that during the Easter Vigil at Saint Nicholas Church she stepped forward to light a votive candle at the same time as the accused, and she could clearly see, despite the gloom, appendages hanging from her throat, and these brought to mind a rooster's or a turkey's wattle, which disappeared when her candle caught alight and the priest cried Lux Christi

                    I never, no, I have always been faithful
                    to my husband and to the church

she would be better off giving in and cooperating as much as possible with the examiner who, from the doorway of the torture chamber, his hands behind his back and his head thrust forward like a hyena's, let out a guffaw on hearing that peasant nonsense about the Devil's mentula and left the tower, headed for his office

beneath the red gaze of Riemenschneider's *Ecce Homo* he wrote the torture request to the bishop, in the event the executioner's descriptions were not enough to convince the young woman to confess and they were compelled to employ those implements on her body

in the event that learning the ways in which the executioner's instruments augment pain until it washes away the world, until it nails the wretched soul under sufferance to every protracted minute, every hour made eternal, every night rendered a long sojourn in a sensory inferno, in the event that learning this failed to convince her to accept the errors and wickedness of her ways

Angela Schmidt, midwife by trade, recounts that her services were required by the accused when her pregnancy was yet to reach five months and the infant was born dead, and according to the midwife, it was the third or fourth time that Anna Thalberg had given birth in vain

but Anna insisted on her innocence despite the horror she felt

Gerda Bauer swears too that she surprised the accused naked on the riverbank, dancing in a circle with creatures barely two cubits high that had white skin and hare-like faces

I have given you blood, the Devil will give you courage, come

she sang, while the creatures snapped their teeth

you shall run the earth for me, and I will burn in hell for you

the creatures ran off in different directions while the accused levitated two spans above the ground and kept singing

travel through field and forest gathering milk and cream for me

in the sudden scattering, one of the creatures struck Gerda on the ankle, giving her a bruise that she showed the scribe writing this

it looked like a simple gout inflammation

nonetheless, Anna refused to declare herself guilty

Marien Bauer, sister of Gerda Bauer and native of Eisingen, declares that she too has seen those creatures, that she saw them milking Blaz Fusch's cows the stolen milk, naturally, fetched up in a flagon at the Thalbergs', the very same flagon that was not found the day the accused was arrested

faced with her denial, Vogel sent the torture request to Mespelbrunn Castle, to which the bishop had withdrawn, rather than awaiting his return to Würzburg

for this reason he sent his lackeys back to Eisingen to gather new testimonies against the headstrong witch

Alexander Koch, native of Eisingen, farmer, claims that the accused accosted him in his sleep to tempt him, to lead him into carnal sin after she undressed, swayed her hips like a panther around the room, and touched herself lasciviously, and although from the outset he tried to wake, when finally he did, it was too late, and he had already spilled his seed

for this reason the examiner's lackeys leaped onto the wagon, spurred on the horses, and traveled back toward Eisingen, and they caught up to Klaus at the crossroads outside the village and left him engulfed in a dust cloud, overcome by a fit of rage, cursing the wagon and the world, his luck and the examiner, himself and his wife, everyone and everything, even God, whom he also begged, after he found the parish house empty, to see to it that Father Friedrich would not delay much longer in returning from Bamberg, and that he would help him put things right

Aloisia Schicklgruber, native of Eisingen, farmer, claims that, pregnant with her youngest child, she suffered a fainting spell when she was on her way home from the market, and only the accused was nearby to offer assistance

she helped her sit down in the shade of a tree, gave her something to drink, and applied cold compresses to her head, all of which, according to Aloisia, was but a ploy to substitute a demon for the child she was carrying in her belly, for since that afternoon, after she recovered from her swoon, she started feeling a strong rejection toward her son, to the degree that when he was born she was incapable of breastfeeding him, he had to be raised on goat's milk and to this day he is a healthy, bright toddler, which only serves to feed his mother's fears of having given birth to, if not the Antichrist, then to his father, grandfather, or great-grandfather

Martin Schicklgruber, husband of Aloisia, declares that his wife lost her mind owing to the potion that the accused gave her that afternoon, that his son has been baptized and there is nothing demonic about him

it is recommended that the case be examined thoroughly.

VI

Nearing the village, seated to the left of the wagoner, Friedrich reminded himself that it was written that thou shalt not tempt the Lord thy God, and therefore he should not seek confirmation, nor a sign of any kind, he should simply trust, surrender, allow himself to be led like the donkey that was pulling the wagon in accordance with its driver's designs, from Eisingen to Bamberg and back again, not once questioning the meaning of these comings and goings

in the same way man should follow the path laid down by Providence without question, head bowed, like the donkey whose hooves at that moment stepped on the shards of clay that lay at the crossroads on the outskirts of the village

the shards that Gerda had left there the day previous, before she had been surprised by Klaus and run into the woods, skirted Drummer's Hill, and returned to Eisingen half dead with fright, but safe

she slept soundly the rest of the night and at daybreak awoke in a jovial mood, to her husband's surprise, used as he was to her curses and grumbles

it's because justice has finally been done

smiling and humming, she prepared lunch, collected the eggs, and took them to the market

smiling, she sold every last one before midday, returned home, and spat on the ground when she walked by the neighboring hut

humming, she made the meal, peeping at it every now and then to behold her work of art, until she saw Klaus trotting along the main street toward the church

only then did she close her door, happy to see him return to the village alone

Father Friedrich had also reached the village and was searching his memories of the doctrine for something to appease his feverish mind and put an end to the affliction that Joachim had sown in his spirit, the doubts and resentment that his brother had bequeathed him together with the sword and the coins, depleting him, leaving his spirit empty and aimless, not knowing what else to do, how to go on, how to muster the strength to rise on the morrow to say Mass, hear confessions, instruct the children, and anoint the sick

endure Gerda's slander, bent as she was on believing that the young Thalberg woman was a witch

how to carry on with his life's daily course in the knowledge that he was now alone, that there was no longer anyone in the world who knew him as a young man, much less remembered the sweet face of his mother, pitted with smallpox

the face that revealed itself slightly in his nephews' features, features that were eaten by carrion birds

thou shalt not tempt the Lord thy God

said Christ in the desert, whereas the Lord, in contrast, never tired of tempting man, of testing him again and again, never satisfied

doubting men as much as men doubt him, in his image

because even Friedrich had misplaced his faith more than once, in the darkest hours of the night and of his life, but until now he had always found his way back

surely it happened to everybody, at some moment or other everyone has doubted that a divine plan was behind the apparent chaos of the world and the absurdity of history, a provident God behind the iniquities and injustices of life, a virtuous Maker behind the misshapen nature that turned dead mules into locusts, horses into hornets, and the crown of Creation into a vile breeding place for maggots

over the course of his life, he had seen proof of absolute faith in just one man, his grandfather, who harbored no doubts after he went on a pilgrimage to Niklashausen while still a boy and met Hans Böhm, the Drummer, the same youth whose name had been given to the hill that Gerda skirted and that Klaus crossed as he chased her, the last place where, so it was said, Böhm spoke to the Virgin Mary when he was being taken to Würzburg chained and hooded, accused of heresy and sedition for claiming that on the fourth Sunday of Lent, in Beghard's cave, the Virgin appeared to tell him that the end of the world was nigh and only those who made the pilgrimage to the parish church of Niklashausen would be saved

for taking tithes from the forty thousand pilgrims who answered the call and sharing the total among the peasants instead of delivering it to the bishop's coffers

for proclaiming that the equality of mankind was an indisputable truth to be realized in the here and now, not only in the ever after, that God had given the riches of the earth to everyone and thus it was among everyone that those riches needed to be distributed

that the high lords should also toil to earn their daily bread and not avail themselves of serf hands, and that the bishop did nothing but ride horses, fill his purse with the poor's coins, eat good hens, and run after whores

that they had no scruples, in sum

the afternoon of his arrest, the wagon that was taking him toward Würzburg got stuck in mud at the foot of the hill, and no human or animal could move it until Böhm finished conversing in shouts with the wind that was whistling over the rise

neither the soldiers flanking him nor the crowd following the wagon could understand what the Drummer was saying or to whom he was directing his words, and when the journey resumed, they only heard him murmur

it is a bonfire that never dies out

which according to his enemies described the hell that awaited him, and to his followers referred to the compassionate gaze of Mary, Queen of Heaven

or the loving heart of Christ, Our Mother

soon after reaching the city, Böhm was condemned to death and burned alive on the pyre, as will be done to Anna, who, lying on the palliasse, in the cell again after her interview with the executioner, was drifting in and out of a somnolence brought about by exhaustion, lack of food, the dark, and the stifling atmosphere, and though the tower servant had shackled her hands at the front rather than behind her back, the pain in her lacerated wrists made her beg the man to have some pity and remove them

but they will only be removed when straps take their place in the torture chamber

the horror of what she saw there stayed with her just as the words of Joachim would not leave Friedrich, who lifted his gaze, which had long been resting on the hilt of the sword, to see at the end of the road the small tower of Saint Nicholas Church in Eisingen

he felt then all the weariness of his seventy years gathering on his shoulders until it made him sob again, until it plunged him into a pathetic weeping that he cut short when the driver placed a hand on his shoulder, obliging him to stammer an apology

> don't worry, son, age loosens one's teeth, bladder, and tears
> well, I am terribly old

as old as his grandfather when he sat him on his lap and told him how, as a boy, he met the Drummer in Niklashausen, how he heard him preach atop an upturned barrel to the masses of people who answered his call, and how, when the bishop's soldiers abducted the Drummer and took him to Würzburg, he joined the thousands of peasants surrounding the Marienberg Fortress to sing, dance, and pray just as the Drummer had taught them, to entreat the bishop to have compassion and free their prophet

but the bishop responded to their supplications with canons and cavalry charges, staining the walls of the fortress and the sides of the hill with the blood of innocents

the grapes grown that year were red, like arbutus berries

his grandfather escaped the bloodshed, lived to witness the martyrdom of the Drummer from the far bank of the River Main, and despite what he suffered in those ill-fated days did not lose his faith, he upheld it until the very end because he met and broke bread with the Holy Youth, and the flames of the bonfire in which Böhm burned, due to some strange alchemy that Friedrich did not understand entirely, only served to stoke the flame inside him, while Friedrich felt his own flame dwindling

for this reason he yearned for a heavenly sign that would restore his conviction, but he should not ask for it, he should not tempt, he should allow himself to be led like the donkey that was transporting him toward the church, when up ahead appeared Klaus, waving his arms and calling out to him

poor Klaus, who hours before had reached the village and, on discovering that the church was still closed, had retreated to his hut utterly spent, but who had failed to accomplish his longed-for rest because the heavy hand of a bad dream quashed him against the floor

a nightmare in which he was still in the woods, unable to find a way out, the pursuit still on, and he was running, not making much progress, as if he were moving through sludge or snow, as if his legs were those of a boy and his pursuer were on horseback, riding through the skies, oppressive, unbridled, ever more numerous

with great effort Klaus managed to escape the savage hunt after slipping between the trunks of two trees, having transformed into a jackal that dashed off, his tread light enough that soon he had left the sounds of the horns, trumpets, and hooves behind and entered a glade where Vogel stood awaiting the peasant, who asked himself what the examiner was doing so close to Höchberg at that hour of the night as he tried to get close enough to lick his hands, but when Vogel extended them toward him, Klaus noted that the fingers beneath the heavy rings were not human, that they were not hands but raptor talons, and in horror he understood that he was standing before the Devil then the lackeys' pounding woke him

whimpering and in a cold sweat, he awoke at the knocking on the door that he had only just put back on its hinges

the lackeys who this time had come to divulge to him the sum he would have to pay for his wife's trial and possible execution, for neither the church nor the city council took care of those expenses, they were borne by relatives of the accused

six fothers of firewood and two of peat for the pyre

a stake covered in plaster with an iron ring to which the condemned would be tied

the examiner's and the executioner's emoluments, for both the torture and the execution

and our emoluments too, of course

in the case of not having the means to cover the expenses, he could always surrender his possessions to the bishopric

Klaus could not believe what was happening, that misfortunes were not befalling him one after the other but all at once, like an avalanche

the abduction of Anna, alone in that tower, her wrists red-raw

the looting of his hut, perpetrated by his neighbors, his friends, lifelong acquaintances the harrowing night he had spent in the woods and his voracious hunger, which the leverets quelled for just a few hours

the indifference Vogel exhibited, and now this affront

but the lackeys shrugged in the face of his grievances and lamentations, they only repeated the sum he was required to pay and set off once more for Würzburg, taking with them another compendium of irrefutable testimonies about Anna's malfeasance, not to mention the little strength that had remained with Klaus, who, tugging at his beard, asked himself how he was to pay that debt when he was a simple peasant whose only possessions were this hut, the cauldron, old clothes, the rusty chamber pot, the broken broom, and the hearthside stump, as well as his own clothes, torn and filthy, stained with his and his quarry's blood

furious, he went out onto the street, ready to fight the first person he came across, ready to kick down Gerda's door and settle accounts with that wretch, but then he perceived Friedrich's aroma in the air and, guided by his nose more than his eyes, came upon the wagon that was headed for the church

he forgot his rage and ran after the priest, who watched him approach, mystified by the state of the young man and unable to fathom what he was saying he had not yet hobbled the wagon when the young man reached him, gibbering about what had happened the ill-fated day before, that she was cooking and was dragged outside and taken to Würzburg, where maybe they were already torturing her to extract a truth that was not true

that his hut had been looted and anything moderately useful or valuable had been carried off, that everything that had not been carried off had been destroyed, and that on top of this the bishopric wanted to charge him for the proceedings against his wife

that the two of them, humble peasants both, had nobody to help them, nobody but the priest, for look how the entire village had turned its back on him as if he were a leper, men who until yesterday were his brothers today would not stoop to look at him

> all I need is a rope to hang myself with, and that's only because they carried off my rope too
>
> tell me what to do, Father

but the old priest did not know, all he could think about was his own desolation, about his brother's fate and the dead weight that was sinking its teeth into his shoulders with the jaws of a mastiff, his only certainty was that the night to come would be hellish, as would the next, that he would not sleep for many days so he decided not to resist, decided to let himself be led, like the donkey

he asked the driver to turn around and invited Klaus onto the wagon to go to Würzburg for his wife, the wife whose spine started tingling again when through the door of her cell came the sound of a voice calling her name

the voice of the old confessor Hahn, who asked her to raise her hood and move closer, to go to him, to eat the soup he was offering and, in the name of him through whom all things were made, tell her story through the Judas window.

VII

In the name of the Almighty through whom all things were made, tell me your story, my daughter, spare me no details, for the better I know you, the simpler it will be to judge your involvement in the deeds you have been accused of committing, tell me, then, about your parents, your childhood, where you are from, what

. . . .
. . . . what can I say . . . .
. . . . what must he want to know about me . . . . my family . . . . my dead brothers . . . .
. . . . . Michael bloated like a caterpillar, in his death throes with his eyes wide open . .
. . . . the warmth of my grandmother's

vicissitudes have brought you here

. . . . Walldürn . . .
yes . . . .
. . . . . . Saint Joseph's Church,
yes . . . . a charming
place . . . . home of
the Eucharistic miracle of the
twelve-headed Christ . . . . . .
. . . .
. . . . smallpox . . Saints
Cosmas and Damian protect us
. . . . why to Saint Matthew
. . . . could it be
because they were carpenters
. . . even so it is strange . . . . .
. . . . Cosmas Damian Roch
Rosalia Sebastian . . . why to
Matthew . . . .

on that trip with your grandmother, did you make a stop
in the woods perchance, did
she perhaps take you to a
nighttime gathering, did she
present you to a man dressed
in black who wore a glittering

lap and her strong scent . . . .
. . . .
. . . . . the warmth of the bowl
in my hands and the soup in
my stomach . . . .
gratitude . . . .

I was born in Walldürn twenty-
two years ago, my father was
a carpenter and my mother
assisted him, both were devout
Catholics, we lived in a hut on
the outskirts of the village, my
father, my mother, and my
mother's mother, my brothers died from smallpox when
they were little, I did not fall
sick because my grandmother
promised Saint Matthew that
she would take me on a pilgrimage to his shrine in Trier if he
saved me from the sickness,
and because Saint Matthew
delivered, we too delivered

. . . . the weeks-long
journey through woods and
mountains . . . . . I saw
the Rhine passing through
Worms . . . .
. . . I saw the cathedral, and
outside it, two queens were

hat and red gloves and who sat you on his knee

arguing about who should enter first, a quarrel that ended in tragedy . . . . I saw Oberstein and its church chiseled in the rock . . . . I saw the black door of Trier . . . but we met no man in black . . . .

. . . that was the time of the diseased crop in Trier . . . . of the witch trials to undo that situation . . . . perhaps it had something to do with it . . . .

no, sir, though she did take me to see the black door and the cathedral, to worship the Holy Robe

the color of your hair raised villagers' suspicions in Walldürn, was anyone else in your family redheaded, your grandmother, your father, any close relative

. . . . little girls like you only bring misfortunes and calamities . . . . . . girls like you have never known innocence . . . . young women like you are devious foxes . . . . women like you are frisky goats . . . . I have been told all that and more . . . .

. . . . she was probably the fruit of an adultery and that is the reason for her ginger hair . .

no, I was the only one, my brothers were not, my parents either, many of the villagers mistrusted me and forbade

. . . .
. . . . they
only managed to have one girl
. . . .
. . . . . poor parents . . . . .
. . . .
. . . . what
does she mean, little friends

their children from playing with me, but I was loved by my family, I needed no friends because I had my grandmother and my parents and a lot of little friends in the woods

fairies, you mean

. . . . . . ginger . . not even our dog or our cat . . . .

. . . . a little girl
alone in the woods . . . . . .
. . . . why did her
parents allow it . . . .
. . what dark power protected
her . . . . the
Devil usually reveals himself
through birds and beasts . .
. . . . the blackbird . .
. . . . the magpie . . . . . .
the crow . . . .

God forbid, Father, no, since children my age did not like me, I would go to the woods to play, not too far in because I was afraid of bears and wolves, but on the fringes I would collect flowers and acorns and I would play with the squirrels and the little birds

and those little beasties talked to you

. . . . . . what do you mean, talk . . . . animals only talk in *Aesop's Tales* . . . .
. . . .

. . . the hare . . . . . . the cat

no, sir, animals do not speak

animals do not speak, it is true, but perhaps one of

. . . . it never happened because when I was

those creatures was a demon in disguise

. . . .
. . . the owl . . . .
. . . . the tiger . . . .
. . . . . . the goat . . . .
. . . . the bear . . . .
. . . . the dragon
. . . .

there is nothing wrong with that, carry on

. . . . truffles . .
. . . . . diabolical fruit . . . . .
. . . . pigs root
the forest floor in their search
. . . if a woman is capable of
finding them it must be due
to a demon's intervention . .
. . those who participate in a
coven deserve to die because
children should never mock
their Creator . . . . . a parody
of the Eucharist, that is what
the Ape of God perpetrates
on the Sabbath . . . .

a small child my grandmother taught me a powerful prayer against them . . . .

I don't believe so, the squirrels always behaved like squirrels, the birds were never anything but birds, and I sought them out because other children rejected me, tell me if there is anything wrong with that

. . . . begone, enemy . . . .
do not follow . . . .
me . . . . for my
angel friend . . . .
will smite thee . . . .
. . if you do . . . .

I learned to find truffles by following the squirrels, that is one of the reasons I go into the woods, as a young girl I learned to appreciate the tranquility and beauty to be found there, tell me if there is anything wrong with that, because I know nothing of covens, I simply like the forest, I feel at home there, tell me if there is anything wrong with that

73

no, there is not, tell me about your husband

. . . .
seventeen years . . . .
. . a good age to get married and fall pregnant . . . . . .
. . . . in that case why has she not yet had a child . . . .
. . . . . . old nightmares .
. . . . human fetuses hanging from a rod . . . .
. . . flayed . . . . slit open like suckling pigs . . .
. . . . . . a flat-nosed, long-eared demon reminiscent of a bat holds a fetus in the air while pronouncing the conse-cration of the bread . . . . .
. . . *vade retro* . . . .
do not deter me from paying attention to that poor soul

. . . .

and you love him

. . . . Klaus . . . . how must he be feeling now . . . .

I met him some five years ago, on the day his landlord sent him to Walldürn to seek out my father because another landowner, a friend of his, passed through our village and bought a desk that he then showed off to everyone, and Klaus's landlord wanted one exactly the same, so we met, he courted me for almost a year until finally I accepted him, for though he was not very handsome, he loved me unreservedly

. . . . Klaus standing in the middle of the room, combing his straw-colored beard . . . . Klaus at the table, chatting with my father and eating gruel as he glanced at me sideways and blushed . . . . . Klaus waiting for me outside the church, a basket full of kohlrabi in his hands . . . .

. . . .
. . it is not common at all to travel such a distance to court a young lady . . . .
. . . . he must have been the victim of a Philter

. . . .

I learned to love him, but even if I did not, he is my husband and I would not be unfaithful to him with anyone, much less the Devil

then what happened

. . . . Klaus traveling to Walldürn every two weeks to go with me to the market . . . .
. . . . the vague sadness that started visiting me whenever I watched him leave at the end of the day . .

. . . . Eisingen . . . .
yes . . . the realm belongs to Neumünster Abbey . . . . . .
. . why did the accusation not happen through the abbey, but instead went straight to the examiner . . . .
. . but the villagers' mistrust must have remained . . . . .
. . . . otherwise it is unclear why she received

we married, I moved to Eisingen, and it was like starting over, the people in Walldürn had learned that I was harmless, but in Eisingen everyone was suspicious, and only in time did I win over my neighbors, or, at least, so I believed until now

no marriage proposals in the
village of her birth . . . . . .

**tell me what else happened,
what has your life been like
over the past few years**

. . . . at first
the women gathered in the
market or around the washtub
would hush when they saw me
coming near . . . .
later they would simply ignore
me and continue talking as if I
weren't there . . . .
finally they started to include
me every now and then, and I
always tried to be charming to
be charming to be charming
. . . .

. . . .
. . . .
. . . . . . the peaceful routine
of country living . . . .
. . old memories . . . .
. . childhood . . . .
my mother . . . . the
boarded-up woodshed . . . . .
. . . the shouts and laughter . .
. . . . . . two fingers, with their
black nails, poking through the
planks and beckoning me . .
. . . .
. . . . . . *vade retro* . . . .

I have nothing else to tell you,
I have led an uneventful life,
nothing has happened to me
outside the usual day-to-day
happenings, cooking, laun-
dering, harvesting, and above
all the Holy Mass, I hope what
I have said is enough to release
me from here

I am afraid not, much remains to be said, you have to speak truthfully because if you do not, I can do nothing to help you

. . . . no . . my lord . . . . do not allow it . . . . do not allow me to remain in this cell . . . . get me out of here . . . . *misereri mei Dios segundu magna misericordia tua et segundu multitudini miseratio*

. . . .
I would like to believe you . . . . . . my daughter . . . but I know the Evil One well enough . . . . I know he hides in the simple things . . . . . . I know he launches his attacks on simple spirits. . . . .

what else can I tell you, I have nothing to hide, I have led a quiet life, there has been nothing remarkable, nothing out of the ordinary, I swear it on my parents, who are now at rest in the Eternal Kingdom

how exactly did they die

. . . . the candle forgotten on the table . . . . Mother and Father in bed, their arms around each other as the room filled with smoke
. . . .

. . . ah . . . . . purifying fire . . . .

their hut burned down last year

do you not see God's workings in that incident, his punishing you for your grave sins

. . . . Mother and Father, their arms around each other, as Klaus and I climbed onto the wagon and left for Eisingen . . . .

. . . . when it comes to God there are no accidents . . . . only substance and relation . . . .
. . . .

do you not believe that everything comes to pass because God commands that it be so, that accidents do not exist

. . . . and who are you to claim what God did or did not do . . . . does perchance your voice resound as does his . . . . the lion has a mighty roar but that is nothing compared to the din of thunder . . . .

no, just an unfortunate accident

. . . . . . Mother and Father at work in the woodshop . . . . Father bent over the table, using the planer on a plank . . . . Mother standing with the distaff beneath her arm . . . . me, kneeling beneath the table, gathering the shavings into a pail . . . . Mother is singing and Father is whistling and I don't know that I am happy, but I know it now, thinking back to that time, whenever my anguish becomes too much to bear . . . .

God did not kill my parents to punish me, my conduct has been impeccable, I have never given him reason for such chastisement

pride, young woman, has suf-
ficed to bring down empires,
how can you claim you have
never sinned

. . . .
. . it is true . . Lord . . . . .
. . *mea culpa* . . . .

forgive me, Father, you are
right

let us take a break, my daughter, reflect and repent, offer
God the dark hours you are
about to endure.

VIII

When the confessor left, Anna lay back down on the palliasse to digest the food that was finally warming her insides and think about their brief exchange, about the consolation she found in speaking to someone who gave the impression of being truly willing to listen, unlike the tower servants, unlike the executioner and the examiner, who only ever talked at her, never letting her respond

the confessor seemed different, and though he had been a little reserved throughout their conversation, she

would take it upon herself to convince him of her innocence by holding up the truth before him for as long as
was needed

the confessor would believe her in the end, for he
was a good and just man, or at least that was the impression that stayed with her after their brief encounter, and
even though she could not see him properly through the
grille, his voice inspired her trust because it brought to
mind that of Friedrich, the village priest who, together
with Klaus, will arrive in Würzburg hours later with
just enough time to pass through the city gates before
they close, and who will end his long journey, begun in
Bamberg that morning at the Colman and Totnan Inn, to
the north of the market square

they will spend the night there

they will enter the tavern and the innkeeper will greet
them effusively, admiring the workmanship of the sword
that the priest will lay on the table

Joachim's sword, which Friedrich could not drive into
the Kürnach oak nor leave at the Eisingen parish house
but which he will leave in Würzburg, in that very inn,
where he will exchange it for a meal, a bed, and two pints
of beer

he will hand over the sword to the innkeeper, telling
him of its sad fate

> it is sharp, but it has known no flesh,
> it has served only as a mantelpiece
> ornament and as a reminder of old
> griefs

its new owner will hang it above the fireplace too, perpetuating its futility, then he will serve the beers and return to his duties, moving away from the two men, who will drink in silence, and after the tavern maid approaches with the stewed partridges, Friedrich will content himself with pecking at a few mushrooms and asparagus and will cede his partridge to Klaus, unsettled by the peasant's eagerness when he lifts them to his mouth almost whole, chewing and swallowing the meat and bones with barely a breath in between, so concentrated on his gluttony that he will not look at the priest when he tries to ease his mind, when he repeats what he told him on the way to Würzburg

what he will do on the morrow to redress the situation

in the meantime, he should appease his appetite and ask God to watch over his wife, the woman who, caught in a light sleep, was taken back to the time she journeyed to Trier with her grandmother, a marvel-filled pilgrimage during which they crossed the forests and hills of Franconia and the Rhineland

they crossed the Rhine at Worms and the Nahe at Oberstein until they reached the oldest city in the Holy Empire never since had she visited cities as large as Worms or Trier, not until she was taken prisoner to Würzburg, although for her it made no difference whether there stood on the other side of these thick walls Saint Kilian's austere towers, the hospital and university, both recently consecrated by the bishop, and the city spreading like lichen from the River Main, or whether there was but a desert

the immense desert to the east of Eden where dwells the Behemoth, dreaming of the powerful sword that will slay it on Judgment Day

the terrible desert where Azazel lies chained as punishment for his concupiscence

the desert crawling with snakes and scorpions, where Satan offered Jesus all the riches of Rome, Kapisa, and Ecbatana if only he worshipped him

it made no difference because her cell had no openings, skylights, or rose windows through which she could peer outside, there was no source of air save for the Judas window

and while Anna endeavored to gather her courage between dreams, prayers, and memories, Friedrich, on his way to the city, tried to console Klaus, assuring him that the wrong could still be righted, that early the next morning he would speak to the examiner to inform him of the evident virtue of the woman

just have faith, we must not let our
faith falter

he will repeat his exhortation during dinner and at
their lodgings once they retire and try to sleep, something
Klaus will fail to achieve, instead tossing and turning on
his bed of straw until after midnight, when he will rise
onto his hands and feet like a bear and leap through the
window, getting lost at a gallop in the darkness

Friedrich, in contrast, and contrary to his expectations, will fall asleep soon after lying down, too tired
to continue seeking to understand the reasons for his
personal disgrace but convinced that he will be able to
do something to reverse the outrage being perpetrated
against these poor members of his flock

he did not foresee that Anna's case examiner would be
the ruthless Vogel, who will refuse to listen to his allega-
tions before throwing him out of his office on the morrow,
insulting and belittling him, leaving the young couple
with no choice but to pray, waiting on a miracle that will
never arrive because Anna will burn on the bonfire three
weeks later

Anna will be taken from her cell to the pyre, exactly as
the examiner was to tell her

Anna will burn, convulsing, in front of Gerda, who
once more will walk the whole way to Würzburg, this

time to see the honey-colored eyes she so loathed burst and melt

in front of Friedrich, who, until the very last, will visit the civil and ecclesiastical courts, spending his brother's inheritance in a futile quest for clemency for the ill-fated woman

in front of Klaus, who will be forced to sell off his hut to pay emoluments to the examiner, the executioner, and the lackeys, and who will live the rest of his days in the woods like an animal, like the old yellow dog he will find dozing near Gallows Gate to the city's northeast, which he will tear to pieces with his teeth before retracing his steps back to the inn on all fours

in front of Confessor Hahn, who will see to it that all those whom Anna accuses of having attended the Sabbath will be judged, that they too will be punished

in front of Vogel, who, having just received approval from the bishop to commence the torture, climbed the tower with the decree in his hands, sweaty with anticipation

the heavy door of the cell opened and the ogre's bulky shape entered, together with the servant and the executioner, who remained behind him, silent

Anna scrambled up from the floor and went to throw herself at his feet, once more stammering her innocence, but Vogel again ordered her to be quiet, bent over her, took her by the chin, and smiled

he spat in her face

he struck her so forcefully that the woman saw the half-light of the cell rend and flare into a million colorful lights

he took her by the hair and lifted her off the ground, leading her to fight back like the fawn that kicks or the rat that sinks its teeth in, all in vain

she was in chains, and Vogel was stronger

he held before the young woman's terrified face the torture decree, summarizing it between guffaws

> you don't know how to read, you repellent peasant, here it says you belong to me, and I will have no clemency, there will be no deceiving me

he handed the decree to the executioner, removed shears from his cincture, and, not lowering the woman, started to shear her head until the hair he was grasping in his fist could no longer support her weight and she fell to the floor

the last bloody locks remained in the examiner's hand and, letting foaming saliva fly, he bellowed that woman is a cathedral constructed over a cesspool, a palace whose gardens and fountains all lead to the same hell

but I can see the filth beneath the
nacre and alabaster walls, I shall put
an end to your deceits and falsehoods

he threw the hair into a corner, raised his tunic, and
kicked the woman in the stomach until she vomited up the
soup she had just consumed, then he placed his boot on
her face, squashing her right cheek as he instructed the
executioner to be ruthless, for Satan's concubines deserve
no pity, they deserve only to suffer supreme pain and die
horrendous deaths

may your hands be worthy tools of divine justice, use them wisely, use them
deftly, use them with holy indignation

the executioner nodded, sure of his art and his instruments, and, while the servant picked the woman up off
the floor and took her to the torture chamber, he kneeled
at Vogel's feet to receive his blessing while he asked the
angels and saints that his work might be agreeable to God,
then he arose and went down to the chamber where Anna
lay motionless, still to recover from the examiner's cruelty,
for not even the imminent torture would be so devastating

because this was personal

before and after, the brutality was not, will not be,
personal

the lackeys' and the servant's rough handling

the executioner's meticulousness

even the pyre's flames

nothing had been and nothing will be personal, nothing but the violence wrought by Vogel, who ripped out any shred of hope, any expectation she had of leaving that place freed from the nightmare and threw her and what remained of her hair to the floor

after those blows, she knew she would never again see the sun or her husband's smile

only surly, indifferent faces like that of the servant, who finished stripping her and tying her to the torture table

like that of the executioner, who after crossing himself got to work

like that of Vogel, who remained in the doorway of the chamber until the torture began, it was only then that he left, chased down the stairs by Anna's distressed cries

but the tower was very tall, and after several steps her screams no longer reached him

on the morrow he will learn that the woman was resolute in declaring her innocence, that despite the executioner's efforts to wrench the truth from her, she did not confess her guilt, she persisted in rejecting the charges, contrary to the examiner's expectations, for the examiner did not believe it possible that the whore, slight as she was, would tolerate much, but the exhausted examiner ended his shift at midnight and left Anna hanging from the hook, swinging gently, her hands above her head bearing the weight of her body, her shoulders dislocated, her breasts chewed up by the breast ripper

he left her there so she would confess on the morrow, so she would give in once and for all and let the Lord's men continue their holy mission

that is what he told her before leaving her alone to her pain, to her moaning, to her unanswered question

why

why Anna

lamented Klaus, lying at the foot of Friedrich's bed at the Colman and Totnan Inn, his mouth full of the straw that was his mattress

why Joachim

the priest likewise tormented himself, why Joseph and Hermann, why did he himself have to drink the cup of sorrow to the dregs, why were pain and death the only sure things in this life, why was Christ's sacrifice not enough to redeem us from the misery of this world, why was man but a fragile leaf being buffeted mercilessly by the gale

but he kept his worries quiet out of respect for the farmer, for it was his wife, after all, who was shut up in the witch tower, hanging by her arms, suffering such pain that at some point in the early hours she will cross the threshold of what is tolerable and will no longer feel anything, will no longer think anything, something inside her will be extinguished

she will cease to be until the morrow when existence will be forced upon her again, when awareness will start to grow within her once more until it permeates her being, bringing with it renewed pain, and the memory of pain

she will cease to be until the servant lowers her, lays her on the torture table, and retreats

> how is it that I still am able to think, how is it that I am still me after that agony, how can I still exist when so much pain is emanating from my body, I should no longer see and hear, I should lose my reason until the pain subsides once and for all, even if my life fades with it

a cold cloth on her forehead will arrest her ruminations, Anna will wince and open her eyes, fearing the examiner, but at her side she will find a gaunt and tonsured old man, a friar dressed in a white tunic and black cape who will place compresses soaked in calendula and comfrey on her wounds, who will spoon broth to her lips, and who, from the depths of his strangely blue eyes, will regard her with compassion, the first look of compassion that anyone has given her since she was taken from her home millennia before.

IX

My daughter, it is with great regret that I look upon you in this state, for I very well know that you are innocent, nothing of this is your fault, the only responsible party is that cunning master of deceit and lies who has exploited your candor to fool you, and who now relishes your suffering, but the moment of redemption has arrived, make the most of the opportunity that

. . . the pain is so great . . .
. . . . my God
. . . . it overpowers all other senses . . . .
. . . . . . it can be seen and heard . . . . it smells like bitter almonds and horse piss . . . . . what does it taste like . . . . how does it taste . . . . . its color is purple and its sound is that of a stone falling into a pond . . . . what is pain if not that . . .

God is offering you, renounce Satan and all his seductions, cooperate with me and give me the names of those who attended the coven, all the people in your village who have committed the same outrages as you, give them to me, and perhaps then God will forgive you

. . . . . a stone thrown into a pond . . . . drops that send ripples running over the surface . . . . slime at the bottom clouding the waters . . . . oh to be a stone that knows nothing . . . . oh to be an angel . . . . to be a mineral or a breath of air . . . .

. . . . no . . . . don't do this to yourself . . . . for the love of God . . . . give in already . . . . take a look at yourself . . see how you bleed . . . . see how my compresses do no good . . . . see how they turn red . . . . just tell the truth and rest . . . . just accept the error of your ways and repent . . . . you will not last much longer . . . . child . . . .

I have already told you, I am not a witch, why won't you believe me, why do you want to force me to confess sins I have not committed, how can I give you names I know not, why do you press me to damn my soul by lying to save my body from pain, understand that I am not guilty, I did nothing against the law of God, I have never been tempted by evil, I knew no evil until I entered this prison, until I came face to face with the examiner, with that perverse, cruel monster

. . . . you will not last, and
that devastates me . . . . . .
. . just give me those names
. . . .
give me all those names . . .
. . . . . my God . . . .
. . . make her give me those
names . . . .
. . . . may not the devil win
again . . . . not again
. . . .

persisting in your sins is the
worst path to take, refusing
to accept the accusations not
only jeopardizes your body
further, but it also puts the
salvation of your soul at risk,
come now, reconsider, open
your heart to God, beg for his
mercy, accept him completely
so you can redeem yourself
and be at peace at least in the
afterlife

. . . . the
examiner's laughter . . . . . .
. . his hateful expression . .
. . . . . . his flared nostrils
. . . . and those eyes . .
. . . . . . my God, those eyes
. . . . Lord, give me
power over those eyes . . . .
. . . .
. . . . let me tame them
. . . .
. . . . may that monster be
obliged to lower his gaze to the
floor just as you humiliated
the Catoblepas . . . .
. . . .
give me the strength . . . . . .
. . . .

. . . .
I will be right here, ready to listen, as soon as you decide to tell me the truth . . . . not before . . . . the accusations . . . . the coven . . . . the sky filled with women on sticks and brooms . . . . . astride birds and fish . . . . on oysters on griffins and on rams . . . . all of them flying around the Brocken summit . . . . .

stop, woman, you cannot deceive me, you are here because your neighbors have testified to your evil ways and your dealings with the Evil One, you cannot expect me to believe that they have all agreed to lie and slander you, accept your guilt before the judge and turn in your accomplices, only then will you be free, only then will you return to the Lord's flock, if you so wish

enough, Father, enough, I thought that you of everyone would listen to me, that you would care to listen to my truth before blaming me for the horrible things I was accused of doing on the bridge, but you don't care to hear me either, you only want me to accept blame for something I know nothing of, I have never flown on any goats or attended any covens

. . . .
. . . . . I never did anything unkind to them . . . .
. . . . . . they, in turn, treated me poorly from the beginning
. . . . they wanted to charge me outsider rates even after I was living in the village . . they bristled if I went near their animals . . . . and Gerda . . . . my neighbor . . . . she hated me from the first, for no reason at all . . . . . and now they are pointing the finger at me . . .

. . . . so many people cannot be lying . . . . of what benefit could it possibly be to them . . . . just tell me the truth . . . . that is all I ask . . . . the unadorned truth . . . .

I am here because I have a deal to offer you, confess now your guilt, inform on your accomplices, and I promise you that the torture will cease, and you will not suffer the torment of the bonfire alive, instead you will be strangled before it is lit, and as such you will not suffer, look at how indulgent we can be if you decide to collaborate with the work of God

. . . . because God is a God of justice and your blasphemies cannot go unpunished . . . . better here than there, where punishment is eternal . . . . . .

I don't know why they have accused me, I can't speak for them, I only know that I am innocent, but you don't believe me, so why continue with this, what is it that you want from me, why have you come here if not to release me from this nightmare

. . . . help me, my God . . . . I want nothing of your deals . . . . I want nothing of your indulgences . . . . I just want the lot of you to let me rest . . . . why don't you all do away with me already and move on . . . . . . why this cruelty . . . . how is all this senseless pain of use to you . . . . . . this aftertaste of raw flesh filling my mouth . . . . . this buzz of wasps numbing my vision . . . .

what do you mean God's work, how can this be God's work, how can you dare to speak to me of God, being an abettor of this whole operation

we separate sick sheep from
the flock to keep the flock
healthy, and such is how we
fulfill divine will, now confess and the torture will cease
immediately, tell me how
many more witches are in your
village, or else the executioner
will return to resume his work

. . . . . . I just want everyone
to leave . . . .
. . . . I want to be
forgotten . . . . I want to
be allowed to go home . . . . .
. . . . to Klaus's arms . . . . . .
. . . .
. . to my parents' workshop . .
. . . . to my grandmother's
lap . . . .

. . . .
. . why are you protecting
them . . . . . . why are you
afraid . . he no longer has
any power over you . . . . .
. . . . . you have no reason
to obey him anymore . . . .
. . just give me their names
and we will take them to the
bonfire where they will burn
for the good of their souls . . .
for only fire can cleanse the
colossal affront of consuming
the old enemy's foul host . . .
only fire can cleanse such a
terrible sin . . . .

not in Eisingen, not in
Walldürn, nor in any other
place did I meet a single witch
or sorcerer, I know nobody
who practices witchcraft or
makes deals with demons, and
I will say no more, it is useless,
now leave

and that was all, Anna closed her eyes and said no more,
determined to ignore the priest confessor, who regardless

remained by her side in the hope that his appeals would soften her soul and lead her to have a change of heart, but after an hour the old man gave up and ceded his place to the executioner, who recommenced his efforts at once, tainting the air with shrieks

the woman is right, it's useless

he said to himself, having handed the bowl with the remainder of the soup to the servant and gone down to the large courtyard where the sunlight kissed his face and made him think of nature's goodness, so alien to man, as if man had only recently arrived, an upstart in the perfect world of yore, a world now disturbed by the presence of this capricious intruder who destroys its delicate balance, the fragile natural order of things

there is no sense in continuing this fight

this protracted war that the confessor was waging against the Devil, in the hope of prizing from his claws one or two of the guileless souls he had deceived, was in vain, he was fighting a war that was impossible to win, a foolish war against an eternal and pervasive enemy that kept multiplying, for no matter how many witches were purified on the bonfires, there were always more, increasingly so, one led to two, and those two to four, and those four to twenty or thirty, as if the world were Satan's royal estate, as if the enemy roamed at leisure through the fields of the Holy Empire and in the heartlands of Christendom

I have consecrated my life to this in vain

a lifetime of fighting the Devil and he was no closer to victory, half a century had passed since he had donned the habit to eradicate demonic manifestations and he was still embroiled in this foolish battle against witchcraft, a battle that had depleted him, a battle that he would lose for good when he died, the Evil One only needed wait until his life was snuffed like a candle in the darkness to continue thriving scot-free among the most innocent of souls

he will continue to celebrate his sacrileges in the depths of the forest while I sink hopelessly into death's waters, which are already lapping at my knees

death would be the end, death would mean losing the war he had begun in his mother's memory

his mother, the reason he had sought to be ordained and had joined the Supreme Sacred Congregation of the Roman and Universal Inquisition

as a boy he bore witness to the power of the Devil, saw what the Evil One was capable of when he fed on innocent souls

> my mother within the boarded-up
> woodshed, cackling

the day the theologist Gabriel Zwilling went to Eilen-
burg to disseminate the Lutheran apostasy, his mother was
in the city, and she succumbed to the temptation to draw
closer to where he was preaching atop a wagon, dressed
in the black gown of a student, a beaver hat pulled down
about his ears, even though he was speaking of God, of
the one true way to please him

> none of those who worship the host
> will be admitted to Heaven, nor will
> those who worship images made of
> plaster or wood, for doing so is super-
> stition and idolatry

he shouted with such conviction that many joined him
that very afternoon

> none of those who worship crucifixes,
> candles, and standards, nor those who
> don habits, nor those who follow the
> Antichrist enthroned in Rome

his mother intended only to take a brief look, but she
remained there until it was over, and when she returned
home she started smelling sulfur in the granary, such a
slight whiff that it was barely distinguishable from the
smell of wheat, but which, as the weeks passed, became

stronger yet, until it infiltrated other corners of the house, even her own room, where she started hearing voices that murmured blasphemies and suggested she do terrible things

she wanted never to sleep in that place again, she moved out to the woodshed, but the voices that had been tormenting her followed her there, deranging her to the point that she stopped interacting with her family members, instead spending her time arguing with those demons and intoning unknown incantations

> wild animals follow him and lick his hands

speaking in tongues that at first seemed human, but in the end became bestial

Hahn's father put a lock on the door of the woodshed and boarded up the windows, and Hahn took care of feeding her and cleaning her filth, always making sure to speak to her, but never getting anything but bleats, chirps, growls, and other animal sounds by way of response, never a comprehensible word, never another human word, for she died months later

> my mother sprawled on the floor, foaming from the mouth, her hands stiff on her chest

he thought about her, thought about death and defeat

as he walked to Vogel's office, to inform him that the woman was holding out

he found the examiner in the doorway of the poky little room, shouting and arguing with Friedrich, who had risen early that morning and, after praying the Angelus and giving Klaus some coins to buy breakfast and new clothing in the market, for he looked a sight, had left for the tower to intercede on Anna's behalf, to see her, if possible, and to learn of her condition, but he had run straight into the barbican that was Vogel, deaf to any argument, blind to the considerable evidence Friedrich put forth to prove the woman's innocence, her poverty, because the Devil proffered his acolytes power and riches

all the riches of Cathay, the Congo, and the West Indies, heaped in a mirage over the white sands of the desert

while she had nothing, she and her husband had nothing but the roof over their heads, for this alone he should let her go and should leave the villagers, whose misery was irrefutable proof of their innocence, in peace

> being, as you are, a knowledgeable, sagacious man, I cannot understand how you could possibly believe that among those unfortunate people live witches or sorcerers

but Vogel would not listen, nor deign to look at him

not even Saint Kilian himself, who, due to Geilana's machinations, was decapitated alongside Colman and Totnan, would be capable of softening his heart

Vogel declared that no moderately educated person truly believed in it, that at any rate the credulous one was Friedrich himself, for believing that everyone else believed when no one truly did, not those who accused, nor those who judged, nor those who executed, no one believed that those things in fact happened, aside perhaps from one fool or other, who failed to see that all of it always served other ends

but he need not be confused, not for that would he release the peasant woman, she was condemned because no one who went into the tower left it except to meet their end on the bonfire, just as would happen to her, her confession would be enough, and of course she would confess, because they all did, always

> do yourself a favor and stop wast-
> ing your time, remove yourself from
> harm's way, forget about this

and with a dismissive gesture he made it clear that their row had ended, and he moved away in the direction of the tower and encountered the confessor, another of those credulous individuals, another of those fools who, so they said, heard demonic voices and saw visions of hell, who spoke of Satan as if he were his personal adversary and his defeat depended on him alone

> to hell with you too

he walked on, not greeting him, ignoring the basilisk look Hahn shot him after hearing him deny the reality of witchcraft and the devious snares of the Devil

> if we ceased to believe in him, that would be his greatest triumph

Hahn shouted as Friedrich caught up to the confessor and both of them watched the thickset examiner disappear into the gloom of the tower

Friedrich asked if he was the confessor, if he had seen Anna, a young, slight redhead, if she was well, if he had had an opportunity to speak to her, if the torture he mentioned would have lasting effects, if Hahn could intercede in her favor, for she was a good girl and did not deserve to be in that place

> none of the villagers brought from anywhere in the bishopric should be tried, the poor are not witches

but Hahn responded that behind every prisoner who was brought to the tower was an investigation that gave an account of his or her impiety, the Sacred Congregation was never wrong, the testimonies were there, he could provide them if necessary

if you were to read the horrible deeds
summarized in those records, if you
heard one or two of the atrocities that
I have had to listen to when those
wretches have confessed, undoubtedly
you would change your mind

Friedrich only closed his eyes, shook his head, and
pointed out that those atrocities arose from the minds of
perverse people such as Vogel, people who manipulated
the testimonies and forced their victims to confess to all
kinds of crimes they never committed

do not be fooled, beware of Vogel

with that, he bid his farewell, and while Hahn watched
him move away, crestfallen, toward the city center, he
remembered the woman's words during the interrogation
and a shiver hit him like a lightning strike

I knew no evil until the examiner
crossed my path

I knew no

evil

bleated the goat, hooted the owl, growled the bear,
snarled the tiger, and hissed the dragon.

X

After speaking to Vogel and to Hahn, to the judge and to the promoter of the cause, to the members of the Würzburg council, to rectors, promoters, bailiffs, and notaries, all of whom were deaf to his appeals, Friedrich asked Klaus to remain at the inn, got onto the wagon, and told the driver to head toward the Spessart Forest, toward the ancestral lands of the bishop, toward Mespelbrunn Castle, where the bishop had withdrawn to rest and partake in a hunt

he took another bed at the local lodging, visited the Hessenthal Pilgrimage Church to ask Mary for divine help, and set out for the path leading to the castle, beside which he stretched out in the shade of a thick-trunked, grayish beech, where he planned to wait until the bishop passed by

he waited for two days, sleeping at the inn and rising at cockcrow to set out for the path leading to the pond, from the middle of which rose the fortification, nibbling cold cuts and killing time with idle thoughts and reflections

the ominous resemblance between the Virgin Mary depicted in the Lamentation of Christ altarpiece in Hessenthal and the Eve on the southern door of the Marienkapelle in Würzburg, which in turn resembled the Mary Magdalene in Münnerstadt

true that all were the work of Riemenschneider, but while the men depicted in his altarpieces and sculptures were made brothers by the artist's style, the women were always the same, always the same

Mary clothed, Eve naked, Mary Magdalene covered in body hair like a satyr, but the same

Riemenschneider's mother or one of his wives, who knows

the second or the third, not the first, for she was already an old woman when they married, not the fourth either, because by then his hands had been broken and he had been forbidden from working for the church, having sided with the peasants

when they revolted against the bishop and encircled the Marienberg Fortress

a different circle from the one formed by the Drummer's followers, they had no dances or songs or prayers but instead wielded pitchforks, hoes, sticks, stones, and a few weapons provided by high lords who sympathized with their cause, Florian Geyer's well-trained Black Company and the reckless Bright Band with no military training

it was these peasants whom Riemenschneider, Bürgermeister of Würzburg at the time, supported

these peasants to whom he fed the bishop's grain and kept warm with wood from his sawmills, for whom he used his textile factories to make banners with the laced boot, symbol of the conspirators' poverty

it was for them that he ended up in the Marienberg keep once the Swabians crushed the rebellion, for them that his hands were clubbed until destroyed, such that he could no longer practice his art

thousands of peasants died in those days, the rats in Würzburg grew as big as badgers

Marienberg remained impregnable and the bishopric maintained its power over the lands and lives of the farmers seated beneath the beech, waiting, Friedrich mulled over the irony that Marienberg stood atop a hill and Mespelbrunn in the middle of a pond, for the fortress was built upon rivers of blood and the castle on a mountain of riches, riches plundered from poor oppressed peasants, first in Mainz, where the bishop's family hailed from, later in Würzburg

and that was the way it went for every fortress, castle, citadel, palace, and residence of the Holy Empire, even of the world over, they were always constructed from the blood and pain of the disadvantaged

but that was how the world worked, what could Friedrich do except wait and wait, until the third day the bishop finally appeared, riding ahead of his hunting party, closely followed by his nephew and the court marshal

Friedrich recognized him from afar, recognized the long, severe face, the straw-colored mustache, the Würzburg cross on his chest, the aura of invulnerability conferred by his continual exercise of power

astride his beautiful, jet-black Holsteiner, the bishop was headed for the nearby hills to partake in a boar hunt when he came upon Friedrich, kneeling in the middle of the path, his hands on his head, entreating the high lord to unleash his weapons if that would mean conceding a few seconds of his time

shoot an arrow at my chest and kill me
if my presenting myself like this has
offended you, but put an end to the
injustice that has befallen the most
unfortunate of your daughters, too

spurred by the nephew, the hunters advanced, intending to grab the old man and throw him from the path, but the bishop, moved by his words, ordered his men to leave him in peace and Friedrich to get up, for the dignity of his years meant he should not bow before worldly powers but only before the highest king

speak now, good man, but be brief, for
the morning is at its peak for hunting
and it would be a folly to waste it on
idle chatter, tell me, what is this injustice of which you speak

the injustice committed against Anna Thalberg

her devoutness, the poverty in which she lived, the absurdity of her trial

Vogel's rigidity

Klaus's suffering, his being abandoned to his luck, captive to an all-consuming hunger at the Colman and Totnan Inn

the elderly priest pleaded for an opportunity to prove his parishioner's innocence, and, even though the nephew categorically denied that errors were ever made in the persecution of witches in the diocese, the bishop agreed to order that the torture be brought to an immediate halt and to give an audience to Friedrich once he was back in Würzburg after the hunt

the court scribe prepared the decree then and there, on his horse's back, then the bishop blessed Friedrich and resumed the march, followed by the entire party except his nephew, who stayed behind to curse the old priest with his gaze and spit at his feet, branding him an intermediary of Satan

but Friedrich was too satisfied by his ambush to feel offended

he collected his things and embarked upon the return journey, convinced that the document in his possession was nothing less than Anna Thalberg's first step out of the tower, and although it would still be some time before she returned home, at least nobody would lay a finger on her anymore, at least she would be left in peace until the tribunal was held in the city

which he found in tumult, with guards stationed in doorways and bands of neighbors armed with sticks and stones patrolling the streets, squares, and alleyways, inspecting storehouses and sheds, searching for the creature that roamed within Würzburg's walls first it was the street dogs

from one day to the next none were seen at the market, the butchers, or the fishing docks, their mutilated bodies appeared later, in the river, beneath hay bales and on house roofs, as if the monster had ensconced their bodies after killing them, after ripping out their jugulars and sucking their blood and marrow

then, more dead dogs were found, several rats, a few cats, and even a horse that had disappeared in the early hours from outside the inn while its owner was downing a beer

the news spread, and so too did the sightings, the speculations

some suggested that these were the workings of some joker or depraved soul, but most were inclined to blame the witch tower as the source of the evil, the new prisoner who had summoned her familiars to sow terror in the city and in doing so pressure the judges to free her

so great was her power that not even the Saint Benedict medal blessed by the bishop and placed above the tower door could contain it

so great was her evil that the domestic animals would be followed by flocks, sounders, herds, and broods in an attempt to subjugate Würzburg through famine

then she would turn on the children, because that witch had no heart that horrible witch

the red witch brought from Eisingen

the woman who, presently suffering violent abdominal spasms provoked by the stork, will lie maimed on the floor of the torture chamber until the servant approaches to release her and return her to her cell, where she will be left in peace for seven days, as stipulated in the decree that Friedrich will deliver to the tower as soon as he enters the city

his cassock allowed him to pass through the gates without trouble, but moving through the crowd of onlookers surrounding the tower was more difficult

in the end he had to climb down from the wagon and cross the courtyard on foot to reach the examiner's office, where he presented the document and demanded to go into the tower to see the state Anna was in and to ensure the torture ceased at once

but nobody else will be permitted to see her until the afternoon when she curses the spectators at her execution, the same people who were now gathered outside the tower, demanding she be summarily executed to save the animals and the children from her terrible threat, but who will disperse when they learn of the bishop's decree

because the bishop's command is obeyed without a word of protest

even Vogel was obliged to obey the decree, but he would
do nothing beyond that, nobody entered the tower unless
destined for the pyre, thus under no circumstance would
Friedrich be allowed to enter, not yet, he would enter it
later, Vogel said to himself, when he was made to pay for
the present affront to his position and his dignity, he will
be sure to incriminate him through the peasant woman
for whom the priest was showing such ardent support

but not yet

he sent the servant to remove the woman from the
torture chamber and then he threw Friedrich out into the
street, informing him that the foolish petition changed
nothing, in the end the witch would die on the bonfire
just as the people of Würzburg were demanding

it would be premature to celebrate
this reprieve, I assure you
now go, before I lose my temper

Friedrich had no choice but to trust the examiner's
word, he will not know that after their encounter, Anna
will be removed from the stork and locked in her cell
again, that Vogel, busy preparing a new accusation against
a peasant woman from Kist, will not go up to bother her
even once, and that the confessor, in contrast, will visit
her once a day to tend to her wounds with his compresses
and poultices, and to feed her soups and broths, but will

not get another word out of her, despite his pleas, offers, and admonitions

he set out for the inn to tell Klaus what had happened but failed to find him there, he had left that morning for his village, or so he had asked the innkeeper to tell Friedrich when he came back looking for him

he imagined that Klaus had heard the talk about his wife and had deemed it prudent to leave before anyone discovered he was her husband

he thanked the man for his hospitality and set out for Eisingen too, though not before taking a long look at his brother's sword above the fireplace, filled with the profound hope that this would be the last time he set eyes on it.

XI

Seven days later, Klaus and Friedrich traveled toward Würzburg once more, this time not to the city itself but to Our Lady's Hill, where a special pass stamped with the bishop's seal granted them access to the passage leading to the castle, and they climbed its steep stairway until they reached the second Zobel's Pillar, which marked the place where fifty years ago the dying bishop fell from his horse after fleeing his aggressors in the direction of the fortress, then managed to drag himself through the gates before he lost his life on the spot where he died stood the third pillar, and beside it the palace seneschal waited to lead the priest and the farmer to the outer court, where he invited them to freshen up and await the other invitees under the shade of the new buildings

they lingered by the trough, watching the builders at work on a new bastion the bishop had ordered built to ensure the palace would remain impossible to capture

they watched the court sculptor as he toiled on a statue to be placed above the new doorway, a Saint Michael in the act of trampling and piercing with a lance the great dragon, the ancient serpent called Devil or Satan, which lay wounded and convulsing in pain at his feet

the archangel was carrying a shield with the bishop's crest, the Franconian Rake, the Würzburg banner, and three metal annulets that evoked the family legend, the one that told of ancestors who were but robber barons living on the run in the Spessart, who every so often met in a forest glade at a stake installed with three rings for securing their horses

the statue was lying on the ground, awaiting its pedestal, and Friedrich asked the sculptor's permission to take a closer look

in his opinion the archangel's pose was unnatural, forced, spoiled by the required frontal view, whereas the

Devil seemed real, as if but a moment before he had plummeted from the sky like a lightning bolt, his limbs lifting when he hit the ground

for Klaus, in contrast, Saint Michael was superb, and Satan uglier than sin

this was what occupied their thoughts as a carriage passed through the unfinished doorway and out stepped the judge, the confessor, the promoter of the cause, and Examiner Vogel, who before climbing aboard had prepared the arrest warrant against old Ava Schwarz, native of Kist, and to Kist had sent his henchmen, to the hut on the village outskirts where the elderly woman eked out an existence

they will arrest her and take her to the tower, locking her in the cell next to the one in which Anna was recovering from her torture, unaware that her fate was being decided in the fortress where Friedrich and Klaus warily approached Vogel's posse, where the seneschal let them through the last doorway into the palace's inner court, a place none of them had been before, and for a few seconds the wondrous sight made brothers of them all, even the adversarial clergymen

they admired the exquisite architecture of the four wings of the palace, so different from the coarse rock of the medieval ramparts, and in the middle of the court they saw the splendid Saint Mary's Church and the well house, both circular and situated just a few steps from the keep, and the sight of this transformed Friedrich's astonishment into discomfiture

it was in this well house that Riemenschneider had awaited the bishop's final decision to spare his life but condemn his work, and here that the Drummer had passed his final days before being taken to the place of his execution

here that those unfortunate souls had waited, on the lower reaches of the keep, which could not be accessed from the outside but only by way of a trapdoor through which prisoners were thrown into the darkness, and which they left only to be tortured or to die, as did the Drummer, who was taken to the banks of the Main, where he was tied to a bonfire stake and made to watch as two of his most loyal followers were decapitated so that he might work the miracle of joining their heads back to their bodies

only then would the bishop believe him

but Böhm only closed his eyes and in his castrato voice sang incantations to Mary that he himself had composed, he sang to gather his courage for martyrdom, some said, while others thought it was how he would work the miracle

but no one came back to life that day

Böhm and his followers died just as centuries before Saint Kilian and Colman and Totnan had died, just as Anna will die, Anna who that afternoon will be woken by a song intoned by old Ava Schwarz, a song of just one stanza that she will insist on repeating innumerable times with a voice pearlescent with phlegm, becoming a new torment for the young woman

> I adore my she-goat
> a magnificent animal
> its fur is a silken coat
> its horns are like Belial

she will repeat, then she will break off to scream like a kid for two or three minutes before resuming her incessant, odious ditty

> I adore my she-goat

despite Anna's protests

> a magnificent animal

despite her shouts and cries

> its fur is a silken coat

despite her threats

> its horns are like Belial

only loud thumps on the door from the servant, sick of her ditty too, will shut her up, though only for a moment, only for a few hours, for when Anna remembers the voice again, she will be confused by the background silence, once more the silence will be pregnant with that gravelly voice that will gabble a story

on Lammas eve we met in the Steiger Forest to worship the Black One beneath the new moon, to thank him for the wheat and the barley and other blessings of the earth, *Iä*, we danced hand in hand around the fire until he appeared behind me, tall, slim, featureless, his skin the color of jet, wearing a tunic blacker than the hole formed by the moon in the sky, we turned to see him and fell flat at his feet, singing the incantation while he traced the three heads of the dark mother on the ground, only to disappear, so that she remained in his place, *Iä, Shub-Niggurath*, the black she-goat with her thousand offspring, mother of the cosmos and wife of him whose name must not be spoken, the dark mother who from among those present chose my husband for her feast and in exchange gave me a she-goat, my familiar, I adore my she-goat she will resume her ditty, will repeat, over and over, the she-goat, its fur, its horns, Belial, until Anna will be certain that she is in hell, that she died during the torture and is now in the underworld along with that crazed voice, which could belong to another condemned soul or could be part of the torture, a torture not of the body but of the spirit, and for that reason worse than all those torture methods the executioner had subjected her to at the behest of the examiner, who, earlier at the Marienberg Fortress, objected to Klaus's presence inside the palace, saying it was insult enough that a dirty village priest would tread his sandals across the Lord Bishop's exquisite carpets without countenancing this starving peasant doing the same

and though Friedrich tried to come to his defense, the words of the examiner shamed Klaus so profoundly that he preferred to stay outside when the seneschal led them to the knights' hall, where the bishop, dressed in a black cap and a tunic with a ruff, and with the Würzburg cross on his chest, was standing in the doorway, and who received the party accompanied by his nephew, still in his hunting clothes

and before addressing the case against Anna that he had summoned them to discuss, he showed off the splendid kill he had made on his latest hunt, a dun-colored wild sow weighing almost two hundred pounds, so large that the game beaters thought it was a grand old boar

magnificent, Your Excellency, you have
left a few Jews with no teat to suckle on

joked Vogel, but no one joined in his laughter

they went through to the hall and took a seat around the table, and the bishop gave the floor to Friedrich, who put forth his arguments against the case, which was absurd in his estimation, for he had known the parishioner for years, since she moved to the village, and she had been a devout woman, responsive to the needs of the church, always willing to lend a hand

he said too that he was positive he knew who had accused her as well as the reasons for that accusation, the perpetual mistrust of outsiders that exists in all small villages, together with the young woman's appearance, for she was redheaded and had amber eyes, but was this not also the coloring of the great Frederick Barbarossa, who, it was said, had not died but, ensconced in a cave in the Kyffhäuser Mountains, was awaiting the moment when he could return to restore the empire to its former glory

thus Anna's appearance ought not condemn her, and apart from this there was not a single reason to believe the young woman had dealings with demons, she had neither possessions nor knowledge, she worked hard at harvest time at her husband's side and had taken ill with croup the winter prior, how then could she have a pact with the Devil when she had gained no riches, no knowledge, no idleness, and no health, the main reasons desperate souls bartered their souls

furthermore the case itself was so outlandish that it could not be defended, by way of example Friedrich raised the accusation of sodomy with Satan, when any person with the least bit of knowledge of demonology knew that even the Devil abhorred that vile sin

such accusations are malicious falla-
cies or the fantasies of perverse men

and he concluded his words, turning toward Vogel, who held his gaze without batting an eyelid, despite the fury he felt, despite the fact that beneath the table his knuckles had turned white

then it was the promoter of the cause's turn to speak, and he limited himself to reading out the testimonies gathered in Eisingen and the executioner's report, in which he swore he had found the Devil's mark

on the woman's crotch, near her ulcerated anus, proof of sodomy that should be severely punished whether or not Satan had been the perpetrator

he knew very well that his own instruments had caused those ruptures, but he kept that to himself

Friedrich refuted the testimonies one after the other, attributing to coincidence, superstition, and slander what the villagers blamed on witchcraft, for it made no sense to use so many convoluted means to achieve the same ends, why eviscerate an animal when you can make hailstones rain down on it, why take the life of an unborn baby and then exchange another for a fairy or a demon, why kill the cows from which milk-hares could steal cream, why utilize methods that kill immediately and others that kill after days or weeks

none of it made the least bit of sense, none of it

that was when Vogel got to his feet, so vexed he nearly thumped the table had he not remembered the bishop's presence and lowered himself into his seat once more, though he could not completely conceal the anger in his voice

> only a fool would look for prudence and discretion in the works of the Devil, enemy of all reason, truth, and restraint

only a fool would expect rationality and providence in the works of the Ape of God, who mimics the Creator, his works, and his miracles, but enough already, instead of splitting hairs, Friedrich should explain why he failed to inform anyone about that witch, why he failed to go to the abbot of Neumünster to accuse the woman who was doing such damage to the people of her village and the whole region, for without question she was behind the prolonged drought that continued to threaten to kill thousands of peasants from hunger if it ruined the harvest that year

why did a villager have to come all the way to Würzburg to speak to me, why did you ignore all her warnings

noting their heightened tempers, the bishop called for composure, then gave the floor to Confessor Hahn, who, overwhelmed by the presence of his Lordship, spoke slowly and hesitantly about the obstinacy of the accused, who remained deathly silent in his presence, and who withstood all kinds of torture without breaking, showing a superhuman resistance nourished by a bargain struck with dark forces, or else a conviction that she was telling the truth and was innocent of the charges

I don't know what to think, she cries and screams but doesn't ask for

clemency, doesn't ask the executioner
to stop, her pride is greater than her
agony

and with that testimony the audience concluded, and
after listening to both sides, the bishop withdrew to make
a decision, and even though in principle he was opposed
to committing injustices, his nephew reminded him that
it was better to commit one than to wind up in disarray,
for freeing that woman could open the door for other
witches to escape punishment, thus he should not let her
go, there existed the possibility that she was guilty, that
executing her would bring the drought to an end, and
in the unlikely event that she was innocent, God would
know to compensate her martyrdom in the ever after, and
would not punish them, for he knew their actions were
motivated by their zeal, by their legitimate desire to watch
over the flock the Lord had entrusted to them

how else, my lord, shall we bring an
end to the Devil's siege on the empire,
how else shall we restore order

the bishop nodded, troubled, and, after meditating at
length on those words, he returned to the gathering to
announce his decision

he would not pardon the woman, but the examiner
would have a period of one week to obtain her confession,

and if she had not confessed by then, she would be freed immediately

he arose and asked the seneschal to open the hall doors while the invitees approached to kiss his episcopal ring

to their shock they were met with the vision of Klaus straddling the wild sow, devouring its entrails, which he was pulling out with his bare hands, plunging his arms deep inside the animal's belly to grasp handfuls of muck that he devoured with delight

the door to the court was still closed, he could only have entered through the open window, ten cubits high

> but what are you doing, you filthy animal, now you will get your just deserts

shrieked the nephew, striding toward the farmer as he removed his riding whip from his belt and raised it above his head, but the bishop, perplexed, ordered him to calm down and leave the man alone, for he had to be starving to do such a thing

then he thanked everyone's prompt response to his summons, invited Klaus to take the minor pieces of game that, skinned and slit open, were hanging outside the fortress stables, and bid them farewell, blessing them and praying that the Lord their king, legislator, judge, rock, fortress, castle, liberator, shepherd, husband, farmer, and father, would enlighten their understanding and assist each delegate to bring this grave mission to its rightful end

the seneschal opened the door that led onto the court and everyone but the bishop stepped through

the nephew called Vogel aside, took him by the arm, and whispered in his ear that under no circumstances should the woman walk free, that the good of the city and bishopric depended on it

skin her alive if need be, but get that confession

Klaus, too, his head bowed, his mouth stained with blood, took Friedrich aside

Father, I think something terrible happened to me that night in the forest.

XII

As they walked through the grand court on their way out, Klaus told Friedrich that he, captive to a hunger that would not abate, had killed the animals in Würzburg, and although he had tried to be careful, had tried to conceal his misfortune and acts of pillage, things quickly spiraled out of control

when the fear of being caught outgrew his wish to await the priest, he went home to Eisingen, where he raised no suspicions because, whenever he gave in to his longing to kill and feed, he escaped to the forest and

hunted quails, hares, geese, newts, lizards, toads, dor-
mice, and so many bats

> parti-colored, whiskered, dwarf, noct-
> ule, long-eared, mouse-eared, all of
> them

never completely satiating his hunger, feeling drawn
to do violence with ever greater urgency, his prayers and
supplications to God failing to bring an end to this new
evil, failing to guide him to the tree stump with the copper
dagger, which he believed was behind the curse that had
befallen him, for all this horror only began after he spent
the night in the forest, starting with the hunger that
assaulted him at daybreak and worsened as he tried to
speak to Vogel, whose voice was now raised at their backs,
obliging them to turn around

> how dare you, bothering the bishop
> for a filthy peasant woman and this
> repulsive good-for-nothing, how
> dare you compare the great Frederick
> Barbarossa to that whore, who do you
> think you are, you wretch

he raised his fist before Friedrich's beard, trying to
frighten him, but the priest was not intimidated by the
giant and his performance, he stayed put, met his gaze,
and even smiled, defiant, suggesting he was but a servant

of God trying to halt the worst of injustices against an innocent young woman

> if you mean to hit me for that, then do it, if not, lower your fist, you're all bluff and bluster

the examiner lowered his arm and made for the carriage, muttering that the old man was a servant of Satan most likely, his determination to save the witch a clear sign of complicity

he would make sure Friedrich paid for his sins on the bonfire too

Hahn caught up to Friedrich and only shook his head, a little embarrassed by the examiner's attitude, and Friedrich made the most of this by asking that he not allow Vogel to play dirty, and that he take care of poor Anna, who was covering her ears and hitting her head against the floor, despairing

> for the love of God, shut that old woman up

but Ava Schwarz only stopped singing when she was asleep

Anna's protests did no good, and the same was true of the servant's thumps on the door and his threat to cut out her tongue once and for all, a threat he did not intend to realize because the old woman had yet to speak to

the confessor, who followed Vogel to the carriage alongside the promoter and the judge, to whom Friedrich also
appealed

> do not let Vogel do your work, Lord
> Judge, he should not be the one con-
> demning the accused

they got into the carriage and headed for the city, and
Friedrich and Klaus walked on, down the steep stairway,
picking up their conversation where they had left it when
the examiner interrupted them, the tale about Klaus's
incursions into the forest until three days before, when
finally he found the copper dagger, removed it from the
stump, and took it to the blacksmith's forge in Höchberg,
where he smelted it and in so doing broke the spell, or so
he had thought until that morning, when the scent waft-
ing from the bishop's kill drove him crazy again, rousing
the animal within, which strove to take control of his
reason

> figures of your imagination brought
> about by your concern, when your
> wife returns home this hunger will
> disappear, you'll see

Friedrich said to assuage his fears, though he could
not guarantee that this was the cause of his behavior, nor
that Anna's case would be resolved favorably, a week was

enough time for the torture to break her, enough time for her to give in to Vogel, who, back in Würzburg, was simmering in his anger as he climbed the tower stair, who the devil did that priest think he was, how was it possible that the bishop paid him any mind and even summoned everyone implicated in the case, how come he had the bishop's ear when he was but an insignificant village priest

either way the meddlesome priest was wasting his time, in the end the woman would confess whatever he wanted

because all of them confess, always

in all the time he had been an examiner he had not come across a single man or woman who refused to accept the accusations in the end, it mattered not how brave they thought they were or how convinced they were of being innocent, sooner or later they ended up accepting defeat in the face of torture

pain and the fear of pain were his instruments, they had permitted him to keep the peasants in check so they would not rebel against the bishopric again, they had permitted him to cleanse the region of all kinds of undesirables

beggars who feed off others' labor

vagabonds who refuse to put down roots and thus never bear fruit the shame-faced who live with their faces turned to the past

and women, above all women, who are enemies, shame, evil, temptation, calamity, and danger

a palace built on a quagmire

that peasant woman was his opportunity to continue his work in Eisingen, that was why he would allow no one to intervene, why he climbed the tower ready to flay her alive to get her to admit her guilt at once, ready to follow the advice of the bishop's nephew, who indeed understood the gravity of their mission, God willing he would be bishop one day

he stopped short on hearing Anna's pleas that someone, anyone

for God's sake shut her up

and with that Vogel understood, finally he knew how to break her, how to make her talk

the servants took her to a small chamber on the lower floor of the tower, even damper than the torture chamber and furnished with only a tilted board beneath a wooden container

a board on which they lay her, tying her down firmly with belts

a container into which they poured water and then waited for the liquid to drip onto Anna's forehead, drop by drop, every three seconds on her face a drop

they left her there, shackled around the neck to prevent
her from moving her head, not eating or drinking, unable
to sleep or think due to the intermittent drop, as if it were
falling onto her thoughts, slitting them open

     night thickens like boiled honey
dispersing them

     the still forest on those long nights
one drop after the other

     a good place to find truffles near the
     river
one after the other

     at midnight, yes, once I went at
     midnight
wild animals follow him

     I found him lying on the riverbank
beasts lick his hands

     I followed the path lit by the foxfire
     and came to the place where he was
as he passes by, they emerge from their dens and lairs

     there were no witches or sorcerers, no
     music or chants, nobody but him
the goat, the owl

     he seemed to be sleeping, lying down
     like a deer, his front legs tucked
     beneath him

the bear, the tiger

> I went to him, I saw him up close, he
> was not a man, and he was not a deer,
> he was both, and he was an owl, too

the dragon

> I went to him, he opened his eyes and
> spoke to me

You need not be afraid of me; fear those who, like you, stood upright on two feet and spread terror among beasts, declaring themselves salt of the earth, the paragon of Creation, the favored work of the Great Creator. I shall tell you how it is: there was no Creation, there is no God, the world has always existed.

This forest, the river, the stars above us: they have been here always, and here they will remain when time, that ridiculous human entelechy, has come to an end along with the last of men, because the world is eternal and men die. Look at the rose blooming again, always the same, look at the toad emerging from the mud once the rains return, look at the sun and at the moon, forever tracing arcs of steely splendor across the celestial dome; everything returns and only man dies forever, that is why man is dogged in seeking an exemption that will never arrive because his finitude is neither punishment nor reward. But he should not fear, instead he should celebrate that such is the way of things, for it appears that man does not comprehend the ultimate implications of his anxieties about eternity: just imagine the perpetual, incessant repetition of which I have spoken; just ponder misfortunes and punishments without end. That deviled life would be hell. Don't you think?

Fortunately for you, infinity and consciousness are not bedfellows. So it is, there is no why; there is nothing to understand.

Even so, man is not content with his condition, will not accept this lack of meaning. He has constructed a world within the world, an illusion in his image, in which everything fits, in which everything happens for a reason; a place where even death can be explained; it is punishment for his hubris, the same hubris that has built such a castle out of playing cards. He fools himself, feigns ignorance of the fact that his world has about as much solidity as child's play. The urchin takes up a stick and says: I have a sword; man places a hand on his chest and thinks: I have a soul.

You need not be afraid of me, for I desire nothing, much less something you do not possess. Your soul is saved, I will not steal it, but it will not rise to the heavens either; when you die, it will vanish like frost at midday. Men are simulacra who claim the right to impose truth, to place somewhere above their heads an absurd God that is all-powerful, all-knowing, pure actuality, and boundless love. As I have told you, there is no God, or I am God; it is all the same. I shall not look after you, you will not go to Paradise. What lies above is the same as what lies below: sound and fury reign even in the celestial spheres. There is no end to it, woman; that is why I sleep.

she ran back home, to her bed, to her Klaus, who woke with a start and asked what was wrong, but she did not respond, only hid her face beneath her husband's arm, not uttering a word, what could she say, that she had seen Satan dozing on the riverbank

the Devil sleeping in the forest

that she had heard him speak in a human voice, that he had revealed to her the truth of the world and of men

that she could hear him again, that suddenly he was in the damp room looking at her, squatting in the farthest corner, blanketed by shadows, purring and discoursing about God, nature, and the soul until he went back to sleep, terrifying her

she was filled with dread and screamed at the top of her lungs, begging them to put an end to the torture because it was driving her to insanity

yes, she confessed everything, it was all true, and she was willing to admit it, she would agree to whatever they wanted so long as they got her out of that chamber where the Horned One lay snoring, removed from the world and its whims

yes, I am a witch, and on Walpurgis
Night I went to the Brocken to worship the Black One, to kiss the Great
He-Goat's other mouth, to receive his
blessings in exchange

get me out of here and I will tell you
everything

which is what the servant did, to the satisfaction of
the examiner, who once again had underestimated the
woman, for he had not thought it would take four days
under the drip to break her will, to make her sign here
and here, which she did with a cross because she was
illiterate

to make her sign her confession and the accusations prepared by Vogel against Gerda, against Kiefer
Nussbaum's mother, against Blaz Fusch and his wife, and
against Friedrich, the latter of which she did not sign, she
refused without knowing why

I won't agree to this one

she said, and Confessor Hahn removed the accusation
in the face of Vogel's rage, and Vogel left the cell in a wild
fit, but he soon regained his composure, confident that he
could get to the priest he so loathed by way of another of
the many witches who were thriving in Eisingen, according to Anna's confession.

XIII

I have yet to tell you everything, Father Hahn, I have saved my last confession for you.

XIV

They burned her on Sunday, they burned her at midday after Mass and after presenting her before the court on the bridge, they found her guilty of witchcraft and sentenced her to death by bonfire, they burned her alive in the market square because she refused to repent for her sins

they burned her alongside the dead body of old Ava Schwarz, who did ask for forgiveness before the council, and for that they strangled her before they burned her, they strangled her after she took Communion, the body of Christ still inside her body, they strangled her after Mass together with her old she-goat, they strangled them both and burned them alongside Anna, who was alive when the fire was lit, but who did not die because rain started to fall

the rain that brought an end to the drought

the rain that returned to Würzburg

the rain that the bishop and his nephew blessed from the balcony of Mespelbrunn Castle, to which they had returned to hunt another boar after Klaus spoiled their previous kill

the balcony that overlooked the pond in which the raindrops disturbed the reflection of the forest and the cylindrical tower

the rain that Anna cursed from the extinguished pyre

the rain that in the beginning made the onlookers smile, for its first drops fell right when the executioner moved forward to light the fire, a coincidence they interpreted as the end of the spell, the end of the witch of Eisingen, the end of one battle in the eternal war against the Devil, whose next assault would be unleashed in the very bowels of the Inquisition

because Vogel was one of them

Hahn will be increasingly convinced of Anna Thalberg's final testimony

Vogel was a sorcerer too, it all fit

his abominable hubris, his delight in others' suffering,

the total absence of temperance reflected in his monstrous corpulence, his contempt for his mission, the threats he uttered against Friedrich in the fortress courtyard, the disdain he had always professed to him, the indefinite postponement of all his suggestions

thanks to that final confession, Hahn had managed to decipher the grand plan of the Evil One, whose guile was such that he had infiltrated the Sacred Congregation to obstruct the efforts of men like him, committed, upright, incorruptible

it all fit

not two months will pass from Anna's execution when Vogel himself will end up in the tower, his subterfuges will do no good, his position will do no good when the bishop authorizes, at his nephew's request, the examiner's torture and death on the bonfire

though Vogel will ask to be strangled, as did old Ava Schwarz

Vogel will let himself be tied around the neck, then he will be suspended from a branch with the help of a mule, alongside the Fusches, alongside Kiefer Nussbaum's mother, but not alongside Gerda

because Gerda will vanish without a trace on the road back to Eisingen after the execution, after the death of Anna, the only witch in Eisingen who decided not to give in, who, in contrast to her neighbors and the examiner, refused to repent for her sins

she decided to step onto the scaffold alive and, from there, hold the gaze of the ogre who had decided to sentence her to death even before she had been arrested

to hold his gaze and smile, knowing she had returned the favor

she had killed him already, only he did not know it, she had taken revenge, infecting him with the same insanity, the same wrong

in the end she would win the challenge that miserable man had decided to pose against a woman who had nothing, who did no one harm, the woman who from the pyre held his gaze until he could hold hers no longer and averted his eyes to look at the storm clouds gathering over the city, losing that challenge too

in the tower, in his last days, he will not be able to stop thinking about it

he should have held her gaze and should not have looked away toward the blackness when it started spitting lightning bolts, he should have won that final battle because he had already lost the other one

she defeated him with that gaze charged with derision, which cowed him, making him turn to his surrounds in search of a place to hide his eyes from her terrible ones he looked at the clouds

he looked at Klaus in the crowd, uselessly straining to attract his wife's attention, which Vogel was monopolizing

he looked at Friedrich at the foot of the scaffold, praying, his eyes closed

he looked in the direction of the red bulk that was the Marienkapelle, in the direction of Riemenschneider's Eve, which suddenly turned into a second Anna, regarding him just as accusingly

he closed his eyes and wished for the hour to drain away so he could find himself on the other side of it, with the damned witch turned to ashes

he opened his eyes and looked at her once more against his will, he looked at her once more because she started crying out when the executioner approached the peat with the lighted torch

> may God condemn you all for accusing me and sentencing me without reason, for coming to the square to witness my agony, for gathering here, like a clan of hyenas, cackling and celebrating my disgrace
>
> may God punish you for attending the coven, because this here, and not the lies they forced me to say, is the

Witches' Sabbath, this is the coven
and all who are present in this square
are its celebrants, all of you are cele-
brating in God's name the black mass
that honors Satan

for this, I wish you a slow death and
an eternity in flames

thus she cursed everyone, not imagining that, years later, many of them will also be executed, that those who will die in the dungeons and witch towers, in the torture chambers and on the bonfires lit every weekend in the market square will number in the hundreds, for once God takes the bishop's soul and his nephew succeeds him, the persecution will be unleashed on the bishopric, and from every village, town, and city, people will be taken from their homes and dragged to Würzburg to meet their terrible ends

the nephew will be joined by other bishops, princes, counts, dukes, and margraves from all over the Holy Empire, on the Catholic side and the Protestant, they will reduce entire forests to firewood to feed the conflagration of human flesh

to dig out those graves in the diaphanous air

the fire lit by the executioner reached Anna's feet and stole her words from her, but not her life it had only devoured her clothing and her skin, had only started to lick her lean flesh when the storm let loose

the drought reached its end with a tempest that doused the bonfire's flames

the crowd ceased seeing the sudden rain as a sign that the witch's powers were being vanquished and began to fear that the downpour might be her final spell

the last hex of the red witch of Eisingen

the crowd fled, seeking shelter from the tempest, even Klaus, who with every clap of thunder lost a little more control and bit down harder on his hat, horrified and furious and starving

even Gerda, who, when the rain clears, will set out on her return journey and vanish nearabout the old mill

even Vogel, who ran to the Marienkapelle but walked right on by when he remembered the statue of Anna Thalberg flanking the door

a lightning bolt struck the pond at Mespelbrunn Castle, the goblets held by the bishop and his nephew fell into the water, and they retreated from the balcony, hairs raised, wondering if that natural phenomenon had anything to do with the woman who by then would be dead in the market square of Würzburg

but Anna was not dead, she agonized, still tied to the stake she agonized beneath the rain, abandoned by everyone

only Friedrich came back

only Friedrich returned after running to the Colman and Totnan Inn

on understanding that the fire would be extinguished without having ended the woman's life, Friedrich ran to the inn, went into the lounge, and removed Joachim's sword from above the fireplace, retraced his steps, drew as close as he could to the stake, and, without the least hesitation, ended the woman's suffering with a single slash.

> God does not throttle, only tightens his
> grip, perhaps to impel you to confess.

ABOUT THE AUTHOR

EDUARDO SANGARCÍA (Guadalajara, México, 1985), holds a master's degree in Mexican Literature Studies from the University of Guadalajara. He is the author of *El desconocido del Meno* (Fondo Editorial Tierra Adentro, 2017), which won the Premio Nacional de Cuento Joven Comala 2017, and *Anna Thalberg* (Penguin Random House Grupo Editorial, 2021), winner of the Premio Mauricio Achar 2020.

ABOUT THE TRANSLATOR

ELIZABETH BRYER is a translator and writer from Australia. Her translations include prizewinning works by María José Ferrada, Claudia Salazar Jiménez, José Luis de Juan, and Aleksandra Lun. Her debut novel, *From Here On, Monsters*, was co-winner of the 2020 Norma K. Hemming award.